Just Matty's Luck

Heartlines

Books by Jill Young

Change Of Heart
Three Summers On

Books by Pam Lyons

A Boy Called Simon
He Was Bad
It Could Never Be
Latchkey Girl
Danny's Girl
Odd Girl Out
Ms Perfect
One Of The Boys
Wish You Were Here

Books by Anita Eires

Tug Of Love
Summer Awakening
Spanish Exchange
Star Dreamer
Californian Summer
If Only . . .
Teacher's Pet
Working Girl

Books by Mary Hooper

Love Emma XXX
Follow That Dream
My Cousin Angie
Happy Ever After
Opposites Attract
A Love Like Yours
Blondes have More fun
and other stories

Books by Barbara Jacobs

Two Times Two

Books by Anita Davies

Stepsisters

Books by Ann de Gale

Island Encounter
Hands Off

Books by Anthea Cohen

Dangerous Love
Substance and Shadow

Books by David S. Williams

Give Me Back My Pride
Forgive and Forget
My Life to Live
No Time For Regrets

Books by Ann Ruffell

Friends For Keeps
Secret Passion
Baby Face
No Place To Hide

Books by Lorna Read

Images
The Name is Zero

Books by Jane Butterworth

Spotlight On Sam
Wild in The Country

Books by John Harvey

Wild Love
Last Summer, First Love

Books by Jane Pitt

Loretta Rose
Autumn Always Comes
Stony Limits
Rainbows For Sale
Pia
The Boy Who Was Magic
Headlines

Heartlines

Jill Young

Just Matty's Luck

A Pan Original

First published 1987 by Pan Books Ltd,
Cavaye Place, London SW10 9PG
9 8 7 6 5 4 3 2 1

ISBN 0 330 30047 4

Reproduced, printed and bound in Great Britain by
Richard Clay Ltd, Bungay, Suffolk

Chapter 1

'Watch it!' the conductor yelled, but I'd already leapt from the moving bus into the stream of late afternoon London traffic before it could sail past Beaufort Street. A taxi missed me by a hair's breadth and the driver, his face contorted with fright, swore fiercely at me out of the window, but I managed to make the pavement unscathed and immediately started to run as I'd never run in my life . . .

Where are you Ned? Oh God where can you be? Don't you know what can happen to four year old kids who wander away from their minders in the park? One minute you were happily messing around with your boat on the pond and the next – I only nipped over to the kiosk to get us choc-ices – you were gone. But where? I asked ever so many people but no one had noticed you – a small, fair boy with a cute, gappy grin wearing red cords and anorak. I searched everywhere, but where do you begin in a huge, crowded London park? I must have looked as distraught as I felt because people stared at me with hard, curious eyes as if to say 'what's got into her then?' One woman, grey-haired, concerned, tried to help but after a fruitless ten minutes or so she advised me to go to the police. The police? I've never been into a police station in my life. They'd be bound to suspect me of something or other and clap me inside or hold me for questioning or – no, I couldn't face the Fuzz but I knew I'd have to tell your Mum and the sooner the better. That's if I could make it to the flat before my lungs burst . . . Oh God, where are you Ned?

A removal van was parked outside the apartment block when I arrived and two men were heaving an upright piano through the glass doors. Bending double, I hurled myself between their legs and the bottom of the piano causing them to drop one end. They roared abuse after me but I was out of earshot before they could draw a second breath. One, two, three flights of stairs and, trembling with fear, I shoved the key into the lock of No.7, forced open the door with my shoulder (it always sticks) and fell into the hall shouting, 'Carla! Carla!'

She appeared immediately wearing her scarlet bathrobe, her dark hair wrapped in a yellow turban. With the light from the sitting-room windows behind her she looked massive and formidable, like one of those figureheads that used to adorn the prow of a ship.

'It's Ned,' I gasped. 'I've lost him in the park. I've looked everywhere. Oh Carla I've looked everywhere.' And sinking on to a chair I burst into floods of tears.

She let me cry without saying anything. Through my noisy sobs I was acutely aware of her silence and I didn't dare look up in case she was having a quiet fit or something. Rivers of tears poured down my hot, sweaty face and soon my cotton trousers were soaked, my nose was running and my eyes were swelling, yet still Carla said nothing.

Suddenly something light touched my wet knee and a familiar voice piped, 'Don't cry Matty. I'm okay.'

I opened my eyes. 'Oh Ned,' I choked, 'thank God! What happened to you? How did you get back?' And clasping his little body in my arms I broke into fresh sobs, this time of relief.

He bore it patiently for a moment then he wriggled out of my grasp.

'I got into a taxi and told the man where we lived. He brought me home and said he didn't want any money. Won't Daddy be pleased?' He looked up at his mother. 'Won't he Mummy?'

'Of course darling,' she said gently. 'Now Matty and I have to talk so why don't you go back and watch telly?'

He scampered away down the long corridor and I followed Carla into the sunny room, my heart feeling like a squeezed lemon inside my chest. This was going to be bad.

Carla sat down. 'You'd better tell me what happened,' she said coldly.

So, standing first on one weary leg, and then the other, I told her about queueing for the ice-creams and how, when I turned around, he'd gone. It had all happened in less than five minutes.

She looked thoughtful. 'How long does it take you and Ned to walk from here to the King's Road?'

An odd question, but I thought about it carefully. 'Five or six minutes?'

'Exactly. So you see how far a child on his own can go in that short time?'

'Yes but . . . '

She waved an impatient hand. 'There are no buts Matty. You were thoughtless and negligent and if Ned hadn't been lucky and the taxi driver responsible and intelligent, Lord knows what might have happened.'

I felt thoroughly miserable.

Carla sighed. 'I honestly don't know what to do about you. Last week you broke one of my best cups and messed up the video. The week before that you dropped the iron and shrank all Ned's sweaters in the dryer, and this week you lost him in the park. What's it to be next week? I like you, I really do – you're fun to have around and you're sweet with Ned but sometimes you are so dotty.'

'I know,' I whispered. 'I don't know what I'm going to do about me either.'

She uttered a hollow laugh. 'Well if you don't know, who does? You've only been here three weeks and already Giles is muttering about taking out extra insurance. He'll do his nut over this little episode. And Ned's so proud of his taxi ride he's bound to tell him.'

Giles was Carla's husband. He didn't like me much.

Suddenly she said, 'I wonder if you'd be happier in a less demanding job. What do you think?'

I'd been expecting it of course but it always felt like a kick in the guts. This would be the third time. Stricken to the core, I stared bleakly out of the window. I didn't know what to say. Carla was right: losing Ned had been downright negligence. If I were her I'd sack me at once, but Carla was special and she was asking me to decide.

As I silently searched for words to restore her confidence in me, the jobs I'd won and lost since leaving school flashed before my eyes. Just like your life is supposed to do if you find yourself sinking below the waves for the third time . . .

First there was Mr Menkes, the chemist, with his pale, beaky-nosed, tight-lipped face. All that fuss he created when I dropped a couple of bottles of French perfume on the floor! Well, I'd just been cleaning the dispensing area and my hands were wet and slippery. Then there was that boring business of Mrs Coombe and the wrong prescription. Fortunately she spotted it before taking any – just as well as it was an embrocation for

Mr Rudge – though she made an awful scene. But the straw that broke the camel's back was that ginger hair-dye little Lucy Field bought. She was blonde and said she needed to go red for the school play so I sold her what I thought was a wash-out job – only it wasn't. I must say she did look a fright when her abusive mum dragged her into the shop to show us her orange head. Anyway, that was it and I was out on the street without a job.

Next there was Mrs Dewberry and her country-style restaurant. There I wore a Laura Ashley apron, waited on table, cleaned the place, and washed up. The atmosphere was nice – lots of pine furniture and bunches of dried flowers and herbs hanging from nails on white-washed brick walls. But the whole thing was a con. Almost everything on offer was bought in from a boil-in-the-bag catering company. The only home-made items were brown bread rolls which would have been great ballast in the hold of an empty freighter, and a few lack-lustre salads. Now I am quite a good cook (a skill encouraged by my grandmother) so when I was asked to recommend the stuff to the customers I practically choked on the words. In fact I couldn't do it. In the end we had a blazing row and I accused Mrs D. of cheating the public with her home-made, home-grown advertising, and she called me a self-righteous little prig and a few other nasties into the bargain. End of my waitressing career.

After that I thought I'd take a breather for a spell but Dad had other ideas and made me work my fingers to the bone around the pub.

'I can't carry passengers,' he said as if he were a bus or something.

You've no idea how much there is to do in a pub

unless you've actually worked in one. By the end of a fortnight I was really knackered. I wouldn't have minded if he'd let me dream up some interesting bar-food but he wouldn't hear of it. 'Don't you go getting your Mum and me into something we can't manage when you've gone,' he said. So it was back to boring old Ploughman's lunches and the usual sandwiches. All quite tasty and attractively served mind, but a bit dull. Anyway a few weeks of that and I was ready to try the job market again.

It was about then that Carla and Giles Robson stopped by the pub on their way north to some advertising do or other. It was, I remember, one of the few blazing days we had last summer and Carla, vast in a striped tent dress, sat on the river bank, a pint of cider in hand, cooling her feet in the water. But it was Giles I couldn't take my eyes off. Tanned from – as I later discovered – daily sessions on the sun-bed; blond, blue-eyed, gleaming with gold (watch, ring, chain etc) and with his shirt open to the navel, he was the best looking thing I'd ever seen.

After a few jokey remarks, Carla and I got talking and it turned out that they needed someone like me to live in their London flat to mind their four-year-old son Ned when Carla started her new part-time job. Of course I jumped at the chance. Mum made me tell them about getting sacked from the other two jobs and Giles jingled the cash in his pocket and muttered, 'Well perhaps we'd better . . .' but Carla quickly said she was sure things would work out. I took to her at once. She has the kind of personality that envelopes you and sweeps you on like a strong warm wind so that you feel confident and capable of anything. Carla has real charisma.

Oh Carla I want to stay. Please let me stay . . .

'You're quite sure about that, Matty?'

Her voice broke into my thoughts and I blinked, suddenly aware that I'd spoken aloud.

'Yes,' I said firmly. 'Please give me another chance. I'll never take my eyes off Ned again and I'll try not to break things. I know I'm a bit scatter-brained but I'm not stupid. My mum says I just have rotten luck. Anyway I'll be better now I promise.'

Her brown eyes searched my face intently then she nodded. 'I think you mean it. All right, I'll give you another three week's trial and then we can both see how we feel.'

Weak with relief I plonked down on a nearby chair. 'Thanks Carla. You won't regret it.'

'I hope not,' she said severely, then she gave me one of her lovely forgiving smiles. 'Come on, we can't sit here all night. You've got to make Ned's supper and I must dress for dinner with Giles's American client. My! What thrilling lives we lead!' And tripping lightly out of the room she disappeared down the long passage. For a heavy person Carla has this amazing fairy-like tread.

While Ned and I were having supper in the kitchen I heard Giles come in but he went straight to their room to change. We'd just reached the mashed banana and yoghurt stage when he flung open the swing door and stood there fixing one of his cuff-links and frowning. He was wearing a navy pin-striper, a white shirt and a discreet but expensive tie. Apart from a hint of sourness about the mouth he looked the perfect Mills & Boon hero. When I first arrived I fell madly in love with him but a week's exposure to his unbelievable selfishness soon cured me. I don't know how Carla put up with it. Sometimes I thought she was too nice for her own good. I'd have told him just where he got off.

It took me a week or two to discover the reason for Giles's hostility which had, I finally decided, nothing to do with me personally. You see, he resented the fact that Carla had been offered an advertising job in a rival firm to his and he'd gone out of his way to prevent her getting a nanny so she couldn't work full-time. But Carla had got fed up with his obstructive behaviour and finally put her foot down when it came to me.

'I hear you ran away from Matty in the park young man,' he said to Ned.

Ned turned to me for support. 'I didn't, did I Matty? When I looked around you weren't there.'

Giles switched his stony blue gaze to me. 'I see. You do realize what could have happened? Ned could have been kidnapped, or even murdered.'

I swallowed uncomfortably. 'I know. I'm very sorry. It won't happen again.'

'It had better not or you'll be out on your ear. I think Carla's mad to give you another chance.'

I looked down at my plate, guilty tears welling in my eyes.

'Well watch your step that's all I can say,' he muttered and he barged out again leaving the door swinging violently to and fro.

I didn't blame him. He had every right to be furious. Sighing, I rested my elbows on the table and stared at the wall while Ned scraped away at his empty dish. The trouble was I couldn't seem to concentrate on anything for long unless it absolutely riveted my attention. I'd always been the same, which was why I'd left school with a miserable couple of CSEs instead of a smart set of 'O's. One time when Dad was particularly worked up about me he arranged for an IQ test and, to everyone's amazement, I came out way above average. So exams don't prove everything do they?

After supper I ran Ned's bath and then Carla took over because she likes to put him to bed. Going to my room I went straight outside on to the tiny balcony, leaned on the railings and gazed down at the traffic three floors below.

London was having a bit of an Indian-summer and the September air felt unusually balmy, but my country nose sensed a storm on the way. The atmosphere was heavy, like my present mood. To tell the truth I was feeling bruised and in need of comfort – because of the episode in the park I suppose. I'd been terribly shaken by the whole thing. Why, when I was so 'intelligent', did I always act like such a twit?

I stood there about twenty minutes pondering the problem, then I began to feel cold so I went inside, closed the french windows and was about to switch on the light when Carla and Giles passed my door on their way out to dinner. They must have thought I was in the kitchen because they didn't trouble to lower their voices.

'I really think you should have consulted me before telling her she could stay.' Giles.

'She'll be okay now. After all Ned likes her.' Carla.

'That's hardly the point.'

'Oh for heaven's sake Giles! What do you want him to have? A starched, moustachioed gaoler like your old nanny? The girl needs to find her feet that's all. Give her a chance.'

'She's had plenty of chances already. In the future . . . '

'Bye Matty!' Carla sang out and the front door slammed cutting off the rest of the conversation.

Sick at heart I went into the living-room and began to collect Ned's toys and put them into their box. I'd had such high hopes of this job – coming to London and all that – but I could tell that Giles was hell bent on getting me out. Somehow I'd got to show him that I wasn't the ninny he imagined. Somehow I must justify Carla's faith in me. But how? How was I going to change when I'd been the same way all my life? I mean how does one? The trouble was that I hadn't anyone to talk to except June, the girl who lived in the flat below ours, but she had such problems of her own that I would never burden her with mine.

Thinking of June reminded me that it was Friday. I generally had weekends off because the Robsons were often away, and this Saturday June had asked me out on a blind date with her boyfriend Sven and a friend of his. Perhaps my date would turn out to be fantastic and my London life suddenly take off. I mean you never know . . .

While I was hanging Ned's little jacket on a peg in the hall I suddenly realized that, for the first time in my life, I was lonely. Growing up in a pub may not be everyone's idea of the ideal childhood but at least you can never be lonely. Right this minute Jack and Mavis would be occupying the two corner bar-stools sparring aimiably with each other, and Tom Knowles would be holding forth to Dad about the latest Test Match. It was all so familiar that it had often seemed boring, but I'd have given anything to be instantly transported there now instead of drifting around the quiet flat trying to fill in the hours before going to bed. The telly, I'd soon discovered, was no substitute for human company. Even so it was better than nothing so I switched it on. A girl with swingy hair was telling us that our dreams would come true if we used her shampoo.

If only it were that easy . . .

Chapter 2

Tottering to a chair in front of the mirror I sat down. The cloakroom lurched from side to side then steadied itself again leaving me with a kind of singing in the ears. It couldn't be the drinks. I had asked for something non-alcoholic and my date had ordered me a cocktail called Pink-Moonbeams which was served in a wide-necked, stemmed glass. It was pink and frothy and delicious. I'd already managed to down several. Matter of fact I'd never tasted a real cocktail, which might seem odd as I'd grown up in a pub, but Dad was strict about underage youngsters drinking in the bar. But there it was the beer that counted. Of course we had the gin and tonic customers too but we were definitely off the cocktail circuit. Anyway although my head felt funny I didn't feel ill or anything. In fact I felt great which was just as well because, to be honest, the evening was turning out a disaster.

It was June's fault. She'd been rotten to Sven, her bearded Swedish boyfriend, from the moment we'd all met up in her flat. Why? What on earth had got into her? Didn't she realize how lucky she was – under the circumstances?

Fortunately my date didn't seem at all embarrassed by the smouldering atmosphere but he knew them better than me so perhaps he was used to it. Lionel Mackin, known to one and all as Lion. The name suited him. He was quite a bit older than the rest of us – maybe as much as thirty – and had bushy red hair with sideburns, sleepy red-brown eyes and a laugh which came out like a roar. He also had this incredible habit of winking at you and calling you 'kid'. 'Like another cocktail kid?' Wink. Apparently he was a car sales-manager and knew Sven through business. I don't think they were more friendly than that.

Anyway we'd gone straight from June's flat to the bar where we'd been sitting around for a couple of hours, trying to make conversation while June snapped and snarled at poor Sven. Although he bore it like a saint I found myself hating her for spoiling the evening and eventually I escaped to the loo. If only, I thought wistfully, someone would mention food!

Just then the door opened and June limped in.

'You've been in here hours,' she complained.

I couldn't trust myself to be polite so I said nothing. Sitting down next to me she pulled a comb out of her bag and drew it through her long brown hair. June was very pretty. She had this enviable heart-shaped face with wide grey eyes and the kind of vulnerable expression that turns some men on. I felt terribly sorry for her though, because she had a deformed foot which made her limp. In three weeks I'd learned quite a lot about her. Although she could be sweet she was very touchy and you really had to watch your step. And she was moody – like tonight. In anyone else it would have been unforgivable and I couldn't help feeling that she was trading unfairly on her disability.

She must have read my thoughts because she put away the comb saying, 'I'm not exactly the life and soul of the party am I?'

I made a wry but, I hoped, sympathetic face.

She grimaced at herself in the mirror. 'I get so mad at Sven. He takes everything for granted. I mean when he's in London we go around together, then off he trots, back to Stockholm, and I don't see or hear of him for a couple of months. It's been going on for three years now. I just don't understand it. After all we're not kids. Why does he bother?'

He won't for much longer if you carry on like this, I thought grimly. Aloud I said, 'He seems very fond of you.'

Her face crumpled in an expression of real anguish. 'Then what is he waiting for? There's nothing to stop him . . . us . . . '

Only the small matter of a foot damaged in a car accident and an operation that went badly wrong, I reflected sadly. I mean Sven was nice, and he must be nuts about June to hang around for so long but frankly I could see his problem. A man would have to be very sure before taking on someone with a disability.

'What does your mum think?' I asked. June's Mum terrified me. She had a deep, rasping voice, wore bold, clashing colours and ran an art gallery. Their flat dripped with these weirdo-type paintings – minimal abstracts or something – most of which looked as though the artist had hurled a fried egg at the wall and left it there.

'Oh she's dying to get me off her back,' June said. 'If Sven doesn't come to the point soon she'll probably ask him what his intentions are. Oh God!' Her shoulders slumped dejectedly then, as someone barged through to the loo she straightened up.

'Don't take a blind bit of notice of me. I'll get over it. Sorry about this evening though. It was meant to be good fun for you. By the way what do you think of Lion?'

I winked at her in the mirror. 'Dunno yet kid.'

We both laughed and her tense expression relaxed slightly.

'He's a bit older than I expected,' I said.

June stood up and smoothed her skirt over her neat hips. 'It's nice when a fella has a bit of experience.'

'What is?' I asked innocently.

She grinned. 'You won't catch me out with that one Matilda.'

But, crippled foot or no, she knew all right.

After she'd gone I checked my appearance in the mirror. In spite of the buzzy feeling in my head I looked amazingly normal and for a moment I tried to see myself with a stranger's eyes, with Lion's eyes. First impressions are important.

Feeling a bit of a fool I grinned at this tall creature with messily styled light brown hair and she grinned uncertainly back, as though slightly embarrassed. She had dark blue eyes, quite a nice nose and a full sexy mouth with a lot of even white teeth. She was thin, with narrow sloping shoulders and bony wrists, and she wore a long, tight, navy skirt, a red shirt with sparkly shoulder-tabs and red Madonna-type boots. She looked okay. Not great, or glamorous but lively and interesting. At least that's what I thought, but what did Lion think? After all he hadn't chosen me; I had, so to speak, been thrust upon him.

When I got back to the table June and Sven, thank heavens, were holding hands while Lion, looking bored now that the fun was over, sat drumming his fingers on the table.

As I sat down he pointed to the fresh Pink-Moonbeam in front of me. 'Drink up kid. You're losing your place in the team.' He often spoke in this pseudo-American way.

'When are we going to eat?' I asked.

He turned to the others. 'Hey the kid's hungry. What say we move our asses to the Indian joint next door?'

They both agreed so I picked up my drink and tossed it back in one gulp. It seemed to explode somewhere inside my skull and suddenly I found it quite difficult to stand up.

'Whoops!' I giggled.

Lion grabbed my arm and hauled me to my feet. 'How old are you kid?'

'Almosht eighteen,' I said. It didn't come out quite right so I repeated it. 'Almosht.'

Laughing he propelled me towards the exit. 'It must be great to be so young.'

'Why, how old are you?' I asked tripping over my own feet.

'Twenty-five.'

'Really?' I twisted my head to look at him. 'The same age as Sven?'

His hand tightened around my elbow. 'Shut up and try putting one foot in front of the other,' he said jokily, but I could tell he was annoyed.

The restaurant was dimly lit and smelled spicy. Lion and I squashed together on a bench facing the others. We ordered a curry which was so hot that it took the roof off your mouth and we dipped into cool dishes of cucumber slices and yoghurt. I don't remember what we drank but I do know that the evening which had started so badly, got funnier and funnier until everything that everyone said was hilarious and when June dropped a lump of ginger ice-cream down her shirt we all fell about laughing.

'This is the first time I've eaten Indian food,' I said when we'd stopped laughing. 'In fact it's the first time I've been taken out to eat by anyone except my parents.'

Lion mopped his streaming eyes with his table napkin. 'But I thought they ran this famous pub?'

'So?'

'Well then, you eat out every day,' he said and we all guffawed like a pack of hyenas. Come to think of it, it wasn't even mildly amusing. Luckily there were no other people eating in the restaurant or I expect we'd have been asked to leave.

When we emerged into the Fulham Road again the night air hit me like a policeman's truncheon and I would have fallen if Lion hadn't kept his arm around my waist.

'Are all car dealers nice like you?' I burbled inanely.

'No. Most of them eat little girls for breakfast.'

I giggled. 'And you don't?'

'Not for breakfast,' he said breathing heavily into my ear.

When we reached the apartment block June and Sven disappeared into her flat and Lion bundled me into the lift. As the doors closed he grabbed me, pressed me against the wall and began to kiss me like we'd just heard the four minute warning or something. I'd had one or two boyfriends but I'd never been kissed like that and I wasn't sure I liked it. When the lift jerked to a halt we fell apart.

'You don't know much about kissing do you?' he said.

'No,' I admitted fumbling for the key to the flat.

'I wonder if you know anything about anything?'

But I didn't answer because my stomach was making the oddest noises and I was feeling alarmingly sick.

Lion shoved his shoulder against the front door which suddenly gave way precipitating us both into the hall.

'You can show me around if you like,' he said having apparently no intention of leaving.

I stood my ground by the door. 'Not tonight.'

'When then?'

'I dunno. Call me tomorrow.' And pushing him outside I slammed it in his face.

Seconds later I was in the loo disposing of my curry and half a dozen Pink-Moonbeams then, groaning miserably, I crept along to the bathroom, rinsed out my mouth and bathed my face in cool running water. Was I dying or something? Very likely, but why? Then, through a fog of misery, I realised what had happened. Those cocktails hadn't been non-alcoholic at all, in fact they were proving lethal in my poor innocent tummy. For the first – and last if I had anything to do with it – time I was drunk. I could have killed Lion! Cursing him, I tottered into my room, wrenched open one of the long windows, staggered outside and collapsed in a heap on the balcony floor. All I wanted to do was sleep, but every time I closed my eyes the world spun crazily and I felt sicker than before so I sat up and tried to count the windows in the opposite apartment block.

After a while it began to spot with rain and I thought it better to go inside. I'd just managed to heave myself to my feet when I heard a mighty crash and, swinging round, I saw that the open french-window had slammed shut in a gust of wind. As I stared blankly at it's glassy face a brilliant flash suddenly zig-zagged across the London sky followed by the distant rumble of thunder.

Wonderful! A storm was on its way and here I was, sick as a dog, trapped on a narrow balcony three floors up, faced with the prospect of an all-night vigil and the grim possibility of being struck by lightning. Something to tell my grandchildren – if I survived!

Chapter 3

The only good thing about it was that I no longer felt sick. Frightened and cold yes, but distinctly, unmistakably sober.

Peering over the edge of the balcony I tried to take stock of my situation. It looked hopeless. There were no drain pipes to shin down, even if I felt brave enough. The sitting-room balcony was separated from mine by a space of about five feet. Ditto with Carla's bedroom the other side. In any case all the other windows were closed. I could have tried to break the glass but as the doors were double glazed I'd probably have cut off a limb in the attempt. No, short of donning my Wonder Woman gear and zooming down to earth myself it looked as though I'd got to stay put until rescued. That could mean a long wait because, although cars were still passing, pedestrians were few and far between – even if I could make one of them understand that I wasn't drunk but needed help.

By now it was really raining and more frequent, more jagged, bluer and more lethal flashes of lightning tore open the dark sky. Every time it happened I let out a yell. I couldn't help it; I've always been terrified of storms.

Huddling inside my bulky jacket for warmth and comfort I cowered against the windows, slightly sheltered from the driving rain by the overhang of the balcony above, and I watched the elements unleash their fury over London. Suddenly there came the loudest crash of thunder I'd ever heard. Shrieking blue murder I banged uselessly on the glass with clenched fists then, tearing off my jacket I threw it over my head and crouched down, vaguely trusting that if I couldn't see what was happening I'd be safe.

The thump of something solid landing near my feet made me raise the corner of my jacket and look out. A broken flower-pot containing a dead geranium was lying on the floor. It must have been knocked over by the force of the wind but – I looked up – if it had fallen from the balcony overhead it would surely have landed in the road. So where . . . ? Then I noticed a scrap of paper half buried in the spilled earth and I picked it out, shook it and held it up to the light. Three words were printed on it in large black letters.

CAN I HELP?

Puzzled, I looked around. No one. Not a bloomin' soul. Then I spotted him, two floors above me, leaning over the balcony. The yellow light streaming out of the room behind lit him up like the angel Gabriel or someone. He waved cheerfully.

I waved back.

'What's the . . . ?' he shouted, but his voice disappeared in the clamour of the storm.

'I'm stuck,' I yelled hopefully.

He shouted something else but this time a gust of wind carried it right away. I shook my head to show that I couldn't hear, and he then started the oddest pantomime. First he stabbed the air with his right hand, then he twisted his wrist and pushed with both hands. I watched, baffled. Obviously he was trying to tell me something. I mean was this a new sign language or what?

I shrugged and spread my hands helplessly.

He tried again, repeating the performance as before. Stab, twist, push. Stab, twist, push. Stab, twist . . . I shook my head hopelessly. What on earth . . . ? A knife? Murder? Twisting the knife in the wound? Had something awful happened in his flat? Or . . . Stab, twist, push. I copied the movements. Yes, of course – he was unlocking a door!

'Yes! Yes!' I yelled, leaping up and down with excitement. 'Please let me in!'

He grinned and nodded then he began all over again but using different gestures. This time his hand moved from left to right then straight down. Left to right then down. Again I copied him hoping to break the code. By this time I'd almost forgotten the storm and was thoroughly intrigued. Left right down. Left right down. Like a . . . like a . . . yes, like a 7. That was it – 7, the number of our flat! He was trying to tell me something about unlocking the door to No.7. Of course – THE KEY! He wanted the key.

Scrabbling in the pocket of my jacket I fished it out and held it up. He nearly went mad, jumping so wildly around the balcony that I was afraid he'd fall over. When he calmed down he leaned over the railings and made as if dropping something into the street. That one was easy. I laughed and nodded vigorously and he vanished.

When he reappeared on the pavement below I let go of the precious key. He picked it up, stuck his thumb in the air and went inside again.

And so I waited, all kinds of horrible thoughts passing through my mind. What if he was one of your goofy practical jokers who would disappear with the key and never let me in? What if he got stuck in the lift? What if, in my frightened alcoholic state I'd dreamed up the whole bizzare episode? What if . . . ? Drawing a slow, steadying breath I leaned against the wall telling myself not to be so daft, while the tail-end of the short but violent storm rumbled away across the heavens.

At last the light in my room went on and this boy with soaking hair, wearing striped pyjamas, padded across on bare feet and yanked the glass doors open. The next moment I was inside.

'I think you've j-just s-saved my life,' I said through chattering teeth.

He grinned. It was the nicest grin I'd ever seen, kind of shy and warm and not too sure of itself and before it faded I'd fallen heavily for him. Funny, when you come to think of it, how quickly it can happen.

Chapter 4

That was it really. I thanked him prettily, well, as prettily as you can when you're soaked to the skin and your hair's hanging in rat's tails, then he left and I fell into bed.

I didn't see him again for ages. It's funny how you can live in the same building as someone yet never see them. Ned and I were constantly in and out of the lift but although I kept my eyes peeled for a boy with wavy brown hair and a shy grin our paths never crossed. I thought about him him though. Oh yes, I did that all right. But dreaming is no substitute for the real thing and meanwhile it was Lion who dragged me round the cocktail bars and cinemas on my evenings off. I'm not complaining mind, Lion was okay – a bit given to groping and heavy breathing but you learn how to cope with that. We got along all right, in fact we had quite a lot of laughs.

Work-wise I really pulled out the stops and my three weeks' trial was never mentioned again. The only awful thing I did that week was to break an old saucer. I confessed at once but Carla only told me to bury the bits in the rubbish bin in case Giles spotted them.

As a matter of fact it was about then that I noticed things between Carla and Giles were a bit on the strained side. Part of the trouble was that Giles liked everything to be immaculate – cushions plumped up, magazines straight, that kind of thing – while Carla couldn't have cared less so long as everyone was happy. But that wasn't all. Something was brewing that I couldn't put my finger on and it resulted in Giles being even more temperamental than usual and Carla swinging helplessly around the kitchen like a galleon in a storm, banging saucepans and hurling cutlery into drawers. Not exactly peaceful.

Once Giles was out of the way though, Carla and I had a great time. We discovered that we both loved cooking. During my last year at school I had done cookery under this absolutely inspired teacher called Mrs Beguin. She was Swiss and quite ugly, with a long, sharp nose and dyed black hair but she taught cooking as if it were a really creative subject. She was a strict disciplinarian, you couldn't get away with a thing, but when you produced a specially piquant sauce or a subtly flavoured fish dish she nearly went mad, pirouetting around the kitchen like Alessandra Ferri or someone. We all mocked her but we certainly vied with each other to create the most amazing concoctions.

My grandmother, who was a great cook, taught me the basics. When I stayed with her we spent most of our time in the kitchen, but since she died there was no one to share my interest so it was really nice when Carla and I began to pour over cook-books and experiment with Indian, Chinese and even Turkish recipes.

The result was a rash of dinner parties at Number 7, at which Giles always took care to play the loving husband and generous host. He really enjoyed that. In fact after a row Carla would often go to the phone and invite ten people around for supper hoping to restore family harmony. In my opinion she pandered to his moods far too often.

Towards the end of October, Dad rang up complaining that he couldn't remember what I looked like and wanted to know when I was coming home. I told him soon, but quite honestly I'd decided to put a month or two between me and home because of this guy called Frank Birk. We'd grown up together and we're just good friends. Well, so I'd thought. Recently he'd been getting a bit keen and I didn't want to give him the chance to get closer, so I decided to stay away – right away, so as not to encourage him.

So that weekend found me, as usual, with not a lot to do. By Sunday afternoon I was fed up with my own company and Lion hadn't telephoned so I pulled on my track suit and trainers and decided to join the joggers in Hyde Park.

I don't know if you go to the park on Sunday afternoons in late October but unless you're there with a bunch of kids or at least friend or two, you feel quite left out. It was a sunshiny day so I suppose that brought everyone along, but you could hardly get near the ducks on the water for infants teetering on the edge clutching bread in their tiny fists, and all the seats were occupied, and a million dogs ran around barking their heads off and picking up sticks for their owners then chasing miles to pick them up again. Honestly I sometimes wonder if dogs are all there.

Anyway there was something rather nice about it all and I set off from the east end of the Serpentine to jog as far as the bridge, cross it, and jog back along the other bank. I'd gone about three hundred metres when I heard someone call my name so I stopped and looked round and saw June's boyfriend Sven Andersson striding towards me grinning from ear to ear. You couldn't mistake him, he was the tallest, most Viking-looking person in the park.

'Matty! I didn't know you were a keep-fit freak.'

I bent double to get back my breath. 'Hi Sven. I'm not. I just wanted to get out of the flat.'

'On an afternoon like this I don't blame you. Do you want to run or shall we walk together?'

'Let's walk. I'm not all that keen on running anyway.'

We strolled on beside the water.

'Which sport do you enjoy most?' he asked.

I shrugged. 'I play tennis at home, and I take Ned – that's the little boy I look after – swimming in the Fulham Baths but that's about it really.'

'Skiing is my passion,' he said. 'Have you ever tried it?'

'No, but I'd love to. It must be great whooshing down those white mountains feeling the wind rush past and everything.'

'It is. You must have a go one day.'

'When my ship comes in.'

He smiled. 'That is one English expression I like very much.'

'You speak English brilliantly,' I said. 'Did you learn it at school?'

'Ya, but I had an early advantage because my mother is English. In fact I went to university over here – much to the rest of the family's annoyance.'

'Why?'

'Oh because they think that Swedish people should be educated in Sweden and spend the rest of their lives conforming to Swedish social ideals.'

'And you don't – think that I mean?'

'In a way I do. It is a wonderful country and it has made amazing social progress. There is very little poverty and everyone is equal to everyone else.'

'Sounds fantastic.'

'Of course it's a rather materialistic society but everyone is into something creative, wood-carving, ceramics, jewellry design – you name it, they do it. Naturally we all work hard to enjoy our benefits but we know how to use our leisure and we really appreciate our environment – which is more than you can say for the English judging by your football hooligans and graffiti artists.'

I sighed dreamily. 'It sounds fabulous. I'd love to go there.'

We spotted an empty seat and sitting down we watched the ducks bobbing about on the ruffled water.

'I always try to come here when I'm in London,' Sven said. 'I love water.' He laughed. 'Even little ponds like the Serpentine.'

I immediately thought of June who once told me that she loathed it. What, I wondered, did she and Sven have in common? Perhaps this six foot, athletic guy with thick fair hair and a soft beard and laughing blue eyes made her feel safe and warm. Perhaps he, for his part, saw himself as her knight and protector. Or was that too easy an explanation?

'Do you travel over here a lot on business?' I asked.

'Ya. I work for a paper-exporting company and I have to spend quite a few weeks a year in the London office.' While we talked his eyes were lazily scanning the scene around us, from the two boys skate-boarding along the far bank to the tramp squatting by the water with a whiskey bottle sticking out of his pocket. I couldn't help wondering what Sweden, with it's amazing social progress, would have done about him, but I didn't like to ask.

'Isn't paper-exporting a bit boring?' I asked. He swivelled round and looked directly at me.

'No one has asked me that before. As a matter of fact it is.'

I felt a sly stab of pleasure, as if I'd touched on something important to him so I pressed on. 'Then wouldn't you rather be doing something else?'

'That applies to most of us doesn't it? Wouldn't you rather be, say, a television presenter than nurse to a small boy?'

'Gosh no! that would terrify me. I love doing what I'm doing. Carla is fantastic and I'm really fond of Ned.'

'Lucky you. You must be a happy person.'

'I suppose so. I've never thought about it. I mean sometimes I'm happy and sometimes I'm not.'

He nodded. 'That's good. Most of us analyse our feelings too much. Although Swedish people have a lot to be grateful for, you'd often never know it. Frankly they are a bit on the gloomy side and very reserved, until you get to know them.' He put his forefinger on my nose and squashed it gently. 'You are different. You are so friendly and you don't bother to hide your feelings. I like that.'

I felt my face going red and giggled. 'You mean I let it all hang out?'

'Ya. It's nice. You smile and giggle and ask me questions without first asking yourself – is it polite? Or – what will he think of me? It's natural.'

I thought I'd return the compliment. 'You don't seem like a typical gloomy Swede to me.'

'I'm glad. I want you to think well of me.'

'Me too.'

We looked at each other with a sort of friendly approval.

'Which part of England do you come from?' he asked. 'Why did you come to London to seek your fortune?'

'Oh well I knew the streets would be paved with gold didn't I?'

We both laughed but he really wanted to know so I told him about our pretty country pub sitting four-square on the bank of this wide, fast flowing river and how, in summer, people come from miles and just sit around quietly drinking and eating their pub grub and enjoying themselves. And I told him about the marsh-marigolds growing beside the river and the reeds you can split and blow through, to make a rude noise, and the house-martins nesting under the roof tiles, and the bats in the barn, and the pre-war punt we cross the river in, and the tall trees on the opposite bank: sun-dappled and bird-noisy in summer, but in winter so bare and quiet that if you crack a stick underfoot you almost jump out of your skin. In fact once I got started I went on and on remembering different things I loved and Sven nodded and smiled and asked questions and never once got that glazed look people develop when they are bored.

Finally I ran out of breath and just stopped. Then I said a bit defensively, 'Well, you did ask.'

Digging in the pocket of his cords Sven pulled out an old envelope and a biro. 'You've made me really want to visit your pub,' he said. 'Please give me the address.'

He wrote it down and then looked at his watch. 'It's getting late. What are you going to do now?'

'Nothing much.' I hoped he'd suggest the pictures or something, but he didn't. He just stood up and said, 'Well I must be getting back so why don't we walk part of the way together, then you can tell me what really lured you from this Shropshire paradise to the wicked metropolis.'

Swallowing my disappointment I said gaily, 'Okay,

and you can tell me all about your life in Sweden.'

He laughed and I noticed – not for the first time – how attractive his mouth was, isolated, so to speak, from the rest of his face by his beard, and how his eyes crinkled up at the corners. 'Then we'd better walk slowly,' he said, 'because we've got a lot of talking to do.'

We set off across the bridge in the direction of South Ken. The wind had freshened bringing a distinctly wintry feeling to the late afternoon and I soon began to feel cold in my cotton track-suit.

'Let's take a taxi,' Sven said raising his arm to stop one.

I grabbed it. 'No. I'd rather walk.'

'Okay, then I suppose I must keep you warm.' Putting his arm around my waist he hugged me close and that's how we walked, talking ninety to the dozen, all the way to the Fulham Road where he kissed me lightly on the cheek and put me on to a 14 bus.

The phone was ringing when I got in. It was Lion. Would I like to go out for a drink? Lovely, I said – I mean it was better than looking at the four walls of the flat for the rest of the evening. So I washed my hair and sewed a button on my dress and thought about the afternoon and how Sven now knew more about me than anyone else in London. In fact we knew quite a lot about each other. Funny that. They always say it's easy to talk to a comparative stranger. Not that I would ever again think of Sven as a stranger. More of a brother perhaps? Well, come to think of it, not that either.

Chapter 5

After the usual struggle in the car with Lion I arrived back at Number 7 at about 11.30 pm. Sticking my key in the lock I put my shoulder to the door as usual, gave a mighty heave and tumbled headlong into the hall knocking the umbrella-stand flying. Brollies and sticks flew everywhere. I sat up, dazed, as Carla and Giles, both in their nightwear, came thundering down the corridor like a herd of buffalo.

'What the devil . . . ?' began Giles. 'Oh. It's you. It would be wouldn't it? What the hell do you think you're doing?'

'Someone's mended the door,' I bleated feebly. 'I thought it would stick so I kind of rushed it.'

'Of course someone's mended it,' he bellowed. 'You don't think I'd leave it like that do you? If you've broken anything I'll bloody well dock your salary.'

'Nothing's broken,' Carla said calmly. 'So go back to bed Giles. I'll help Matty clear this lot up.'

He fumed away down the passage and Carla and I cleared up the hall.

'I'm sorry,' I said. 'It really was sticking when I went out.'

Carla returned the golfing umbrella to the stand. 'I know. He re-hung it this evening. I should have left a note on the door. Did you have a good weekend?'

'Quite. Did you?'

'So-so. Giles wasn't in a very good mood, and because my mother likes everyone to be happy, we all had to pretend that nothing was wrong. That can be a bit of a strain sometimes. By the way Ned's cold is better.'

'Great. I'll take him swimming after nursery-school.' At my bedroom door I turned. 'Carla, why does Giles get so mad at me all the time?'

She sagged against the wall. 'Oh Matty, it's not just you. It's me, Ned, everyone. I wish I knew the answer.'

She looked so forlorn that I wanted to put my arms around her and comfort her but I didn't. You don't, do you? Not when it's your employer.

During the next week or two things between Carla and Giles definitely took a turn for the worse. The atmosphere in the evenings was awful and I did my best to get Ned into bed before Giles came home because all he ever did was criticize him. Once, when Carla was tucking him in for the night I heard Ned ask, 'Mummy, why is Daddy always cross?' and I thought – they're going to have problems with him if they don't watch out.

Wednesday was one of my free nights and, if her mother was out, I sometimes had supper with June. By this time I'd got to know her better and, to be honest, I felt incredibly sorry for her. We never talked about her deformed foot and I never saw it out of its surgical shoe. All I knew was that she'd had this accident, involving a drunk driver, while crossing the road when she was thirteen and successive operations had failed to put things right.

I think she'd given up the struggle for independence. She lived with her mother who seemed quite happy to let her lounge around all day doing nothing. Sometimes, when they were short of staff, she did a brief stint in Mrs Belasco's art gallery, and now and then she disappeared off to Paris or Florence or somewhere to stay with friends. I'd never met anyone who didn't have to work for their living so it was quite a revelation.

The trouble was, her life lacked a focal point. She was bored and unhappy. I mean if you don't actually need to get out of bed in the morning in order to go to work, feed the baby, tune your tuba, or whatever, well, unless you are the self-motivated type, you don't bother.

June really needed a proper job and I think she knew it but couldn't muster the energy or the confidence to override her disability and break away from home.

June's mother's flat was, in my opinion, totally bizarre. It was just like an art gallery. Everything was stark white – even the carpet, only that had squiggly black and red lines all over it. There were no curtains to soften the windows and no cushions to brighten the black leather sofas and chairs in the huge, bleak living-room. There was a forest of brilliant spot-lights which focused on the weird pictures and bits of twisted metal and sculpted stone on the tables. I knew for a fact that June's mum often brought clients home and flogged the displayed art-work to them over cocktails and Bombay-mix. Home sweet home eh?

Mrs Belasco came out of the flat as I went in. She was wearing dark glasses, orange jacket, purple skirt, black shoes and tights and she looked like a cartoon witch.

'Hallo darling,' she rasped, enveloping me in clouds of cigar smoke. 'You must cheer up my poor baby. She's rather in the dumps this evening. Can't imagine why. After all, it's a wonderful chance.'

'It is?' What on earth was she babbling about?

'Well of course it is angel. There's champagne in the

kitchen. Help yourselves. Go on celebrate!' And off she went.

I found June stretched out on a black sofa wearing white trousers and a glitzy top. She looked stunning. If she'd told me we were dressing up to eat our supper in front of the telly I'd at least have put on some lipstick but in my old jeans and checked shirt I felt rather like an assistant window-dresser arriving to check the display.

'Your mother says to open the champagne,' I said.

She waved a languid hand towards the kitchen. 'Why not?'

I fetched the bottle and managed to pop the cork without losing too much fizz and poured us a glass each and sat down. Mrs Belasco was right, June did look depressed.

'What are we supposed to be celebrating?'

'Mother's imminent liberation from her crippled daughter,' she said bitterly. 'She thinks she's found a surgeon who can do something about my foot.'

'But that's marvellous.'

'You wouldn't think so if you'd already had three operations none of which had worked.'

'Then what's different about this one?'

June shrugged. 'Lord knows. It's a new technique they've perfected in the States. I'd have to go there for the op. and stay there for quite a while under this particular doctor – otherwise he won't attempt it.'

'Would you be able to wear proper shoes afterwards and walk normally and everything?'

'He seems to think so.'

'Well then, isn't it worth a try?'

She threw back her head and closed her eyes. 'God

I'm sick of doctors! I'm used to the way I am now. Why can't I just stay like it?'

'I suppose you can. It can't be much fun though.'

'Fun!' She opened her eyes and looked at me. 'Do you know when I last remember having fun? When I was twelve and some of us ran away from our teacher in Windsor Great Park. Even now I can feel the strength in my legs as I flew over the grass with the others leaving the old bag shouting her head off . . . Six weeks later I was in hospital.'

'Perhaps you'll be able to do that again – run, I mean.'

'Yeah. And pigs might fly!'

She was in a terrible mood – one of her worst. Half of me wanted to get up and leave but the other half realized she was really unhappy and wanted to help.

'Are you worried about leaving Sven?' I asked.

She nodded. 'I kind of depend on him. But it isn't only that – or even the bore of yet another op. You see I'd have to live with my father and stepmother and I hardly know her. She's very sweet and all that but it's quite easy to be nice to someone you won't see again for a year or two. It's different when they have to live with you. Suppose we don't get along? Suppose I hate her?'

'Suppose you make up your mind to like her?' I said gently.

She gave a dry little laugh. 'You're a much nicer person than I am Matty.'

'I gather your mother thinks it a great idea but what does Sven think?'

'I don't know yet. I'll ask him later, when you've gone.'

I jumped up. 'You didn't tell me he was coming!'

She looked surprised. 'What difference does it make?'

'I er . . . none I suppose.' But it did, although I couldn't have explained why. Perhaps it had something to do with me looking a mess and June looking so bril; perhaps I was a teeny bit reluctant to see them together when Sven and I had seemed so close that afternoon in the park. 'I'd better leave you alone,' I said, my heart thumping madly.

June groaned. 'Don't be so daft. You've come for supper haven't you?'

When Sven arrived, he filled Mrs B's echoing hall with a kind of electric energy. Holding me at arm's length he boomed. 'Matty! You glow like a daffodil in these arctic surroundings.'

'Ssh.'

'Why ssh?' June knows exactly what I think of her mother's taste in interior design.'

'Mother knows it too,' June said drily.

I handed Sven a glass of champagne. 'With Mrs Belasco's compliments.'

He laughed. 'You're a great liar Matty. Skol!'

He then got the record player going and we sat around listening to Peter Gabriel and yakking about this and that. Or, rather Sven and I did. June just lay there not contributing to the conversation or, as far as I could tell, even listening to it. Minutes earlier she had been discussing her life in a reasonably animated way but now, for no reason, she'd just opted out. Frankly I could have kicked her.

Sven was different too. Although he laughed and joked, he seemed ill at ease and I couldn't help marvelling at the way people complicate their lives. With the decision about the op. looming, June needed Sven more than ever but she was either too proud, or too intent on getting back at him for some imagined slight, to show it.

After we'd finished the champagne Sven announced that he was starved and dragged me off to the kitchen. June vaguely offered to help but that was as far as it went. A pre-cooked spaghetti-bolognese was sitting on top of the cooker so I shoved it inside and got on with preparing a salad while Sven made the dressing.

'I don't know why Matty and I should do this,' he grumbled loudly but humorously. 'After all you invited us to supper.'

June's dry little laugh issued from the living room. 'I suppose I'm just lazy.'

'It's a good thing Matty's not lazy,' he said vigorously whisking the oil and lemon juice.

'Oh but I am,' I laughed. 'Luckily you don't know me.'

We were standing each side of the kitchen table and as I spoke I looked up, straight into his now serious eyes.

'On the contrary. I know you well.'

Quite suddenly I felt as though I'd stuck my finger into a live electric socket. The most extraordinary feeling zoomed up and down my spine and for a couple of paralysing seconds I could only stare back, lost in the blue depths of his gaze. Then he looked down and I shook myself, like a dog coming out of the sea, and everything returned to normal.

Towards the end of the meal Sven announced that he had to go back to Stockholm on Monday.

June made a face. 'Again? How long for this time?'

'A couple of weeks. My brother will be returning with me.'

'Would he do for Matty?'

'June!' I protested blushing furiously.

'Well, you're too good for Lion.'

'I'm afraid not,' Sven said. 'He's coming over to get married.'

There was a short burst of silence. Like gunfire.

'I see,' June said crisply. 'Then he won't I suppose.'

'Anyway I've got a boyfriend at home,' I lied nervously. Anything to change the delicate subject.

'You sly thing!' June said. 'What's he like?'

I thought of Frank Birk's great shambling body and red face. 'Kind of large – around the girth I mean – like a shire horse. And he gives me amazing presents.' I could see they didn't know whether or not to take me seriously.

June's eyes lit up. 'What sort of things? Don't keep us in suspense.'

'Guess.'

They looked at each other. 'Hand made chocs?' June suggested. 'Orchids? Diamond bracelets? Trips to Hong Kong?'

Sven joined in. 'Cars? Boats? Helicopters?'

'Give up?'

'Yes!' they chorused.

'Liver, sausages, and pigs' trotters. He's a butcher.'

They both burst out laughing. I felt a momentary pang of conscience about poor old Frank but at least I'd managed to divert June and saved Sven's evening for him. His remark about his brother's marriage could have provoked one of June's blackest moods. Now I could leave them to discuss her proposed operation rationally.

Sven came to the door with me. 'You can do better than a shire horse Matty.'

'Yeah I know. Lion.'

'God no! Much better than him. You've got a lot going for you. Don't forget it.'

'Thanks Sven,' I kissed his cheek, and his beard tickled my mouth. Dear Sven. Now there was a really nice guy. No wonder June wanted to nail him for ever.

When the lift arrived, I got in.

'Hi.'

I looked round. Propped against the wall, half hidden behind a box overflowing with groceries stood the boy who had rescued me from the balcony on the night of the storm. My hero.

Chapter 6

Then the lift jerked into life and the oranges piled on top of the box promptly disgorged on to the coconut matting.

'I'll get them,' I said.

'Thanks.' Resting his foot against the opposite wall he balanced the box on his outstretched leg. 'I hate shopping so I only do it once a month. Usually there's no one around to pick up the stuff.'

'Oh well, tit for tat,' I said, ineptly juggling a dozen oranges. 'After all I do owe you my life.'

He grinned. 'So you do.'

Oh I'd dreamed about that grin!

He eyed the oranges doubtfully. 'There doesn't seem

to be much room in the box for those.'

Dad was always going on about making the most of your opportunities. Well, now was my chance.

'Don't worry,' I said casually. 'I'll dump them in your flat for you.'

It had all happened so fast. Since the episode on the balcony I'd kept an eagle eye open but hadn't glimpsed a hair of his head and now, suddenly, here he was needing my help. Ain't life amazin'?

'Sorry about the mess,' he said when we walked into the flat, 'but my parents are away and housekeeping isn't my strong point.'

You could say that again! The kitchen – more old fashioned than my gran's had been – was literally covered with dirty pots and pans. It smelt too. I guessed he hadn't emptied the rubbish bin for days.

He cleared a space on the table and put down the groceries while I looked around for somewhere to put the oranges.

'Here give them to me,' he said.

I tried, but between us we managed to drop most of them.

'Leave them,' he laughed. 'I'll pick them up later.'

'Okay.' I grinned and sort of backed towards the door. I didn't want to go so soon but I couldn't stay unless he . . .

'Fancy a coffee?'

I breathed again. 'Yeah. Why not?'

'Right. You go into the drawing-room and I'll make some. I'm so incompetent that I hate being watched.'

So I went, leaving him to play hide and seek among the dirty pans.

The drawing-room (definitely not a 'sitting' or a 'living' room) had a parquet floor spread with beautiful but faded rugs, and sofas and chairs covered in rich, but worn velvets. Tapestries and big mirrors adorned the walls and there were a lot of antique tables and statues and things.

Plonking myself in the corner of a velvet sofa which was kind of looped together at the corners with tassled cords, I closed my eyes and relaxed, still hardly able to believe my luck. The room felt lovely: peaceful and soothing – an amazing contrast to Mrs Belasco's stark apartment and Carla's untidy flat. Here you felt people often sat and talked about interesting, important things – world events and the like. So I just lay back, soaking up the atmosphere, and waited for my hero to bring me refreshment. Coffee from the Orient and a tray of delicious sticky sweetmeats . . . ?

No such luck. He finally appeared with a couple of mugs of the instant stuff and a packet of Jaffa Cakes. Sitting down next to me he handed me a mug.

'I don't know your name. Mine's Harry. Harry Lord.'

'Matty Davies.'

'You look after the Robson's little boy don't you?'

'Yeah. He's sweet.' I looked around. 'Lovely flat you've got. Do you live here alone? Where are your parents?' It may have sounded nosy but it might be ages before I saw him again. Anyway he didn't seem to mind.

'In Germany. My father's in the Foreign Office.'

'So what do you do?'

'I'm studying to re-take my As. Then I hope to go to medical school.' He grimaced wryly. 'I need better grades you see.'

I shuddered. 'I can't imagine being a doctor – all that blood and stuff. Have you always wanted to be one?'

'Yes. I find it very interesting and I like looking after people. It's the only thing I've ever wanted to do. In fact I can't imagine doing anything else.'

'What if you don't make it?'

He groaned. 'I'll probably commit suicide.'

I giggled. 'Really? How?'

'Oh I don't know.' He blew thoughtfully on to his hot coffee. 'Shouldn't be too difficult. Westminster Bridge is tempting. Have you noticed?'

'Can't say I have.' This was turning into a funny sort of conversation, and not funny ha-ha either.

He turned his head and looked at me, sort of sizing me up.

'No I don't suppose you have, but then I don't suppose you are desperately in love.'

'Why, are you?'

He sighed. 'Yes. Unfortunately.'

For several moments neither of us spoke. I suppose he was thinking about his unrequited love and I was busy coming to terms with my disappointment. I could hardly believe that I'd finally met him only to learn that he was in love with someone else. Could Fate be so cruel?

I glanced sideways. He was staring gloomily down at his Jaffa cake – a case of love-sickness if ever I saw one. You'd never have called him good-looking – not like June's Sven – but he had a nice face, round and pink-cheeked, with thoughtful brown eyes. His hair was brown too, and wavy, and it kind of stuck up at the back. In fact he looked endearingly schoolboyish from the top of his head down to his Vyella checked shirt, beige cords and his scruffy moccasins. At the same time he was amazingly attractive and, for anything, I'd have put my arms around him and told him not to waste himself on this other girl but to take a look at the local talent. I didn't though. I mean you don't, do you – not when you've just met a guy and you're sitting on his mother's antique sofa?

'What's she like?' I asked – not really wanting to know.

He groaned again but even more rendingly. 'Beautiful. God she's absolutely beautiful.'

'Does she fancy you too?'

He ran his hand distractedly through his hair. 'Yes. No. I don't know. That's the trouble. It's driving me spare.'

'What's her name?'

'Diane. Diane Parks. She's an actress.'

It was getting worse and worse. I mean how could you compete with a beautiful actress called Diane?

'Is she acting in something now?'

'No. She's still at drama school but I expect she'll be snapped up for television or something before she's finished. She's amazingly talented.'

'So why are you in such a state?'

'A state? Who said I was in a state?'

'Aren't you? Well you could have fooled me!'

Ignoring his annoyance I gazed at the portrait of a lady in flowing robes sporting Prince of Wales feathers in her hair, which was hanging over the fireplace.

'My great grandmother,' Harry said.

I nodded. She had his nose – or he had hers. Anyway it looked better on him.

'Oh well I suppose I am,' he admitted suddenly. 'Diane is impossible. I never know where I am with her. First she says she'll come to supper and doesn't turn up. Then she says she never wants to see me again and I find her waiting for me, shivering with cold outside my college. I just don't know what to make of her. I know she goes out with other men.' He sighed deeply. 'I expect I'm jealous.'

'Yeah. I'd say you are.'

He'd got it badly, really badly. It was clear I could either give up immediately or play a waiting game and hope to be around to pick up the pieces if things fell apart. After all I had nothing to lose . . . except my heart . . . except my heart . . .

So there we sat, munching our biscuits, and after a bit he kind of shook his head as if to shoo away the blues and said,

'Sorry I'm such rotten company. Let's have some music to cheer ourselves up.' He disappeared into a dim corner and the next minute the familiar strains of Simple Minds filled the room.

'Great!' I said. 'I'm mad about Jim Kerr.'

'Thought you would be. Diane is too.'

'Really?' I sighed inwardly, wondering if everything we talked about would somehow find its way back to Diane.

Shoving aside a table covered with photographs of the late Shah of Persia and various Presidents of the USA, he began snapping his fingers to the music and jerking around the room.

'Come on Matty – let's move!'

I'd like to be able to say that he danced well, but, truth be told, he was awful. He totally lacked a sense of rhythm and charged about the place flinging up his arms and stamping his feet like the proverbial bull in a china shop. It was really funny. It was also rather sweet because he thought he was being amazingly hip. The great thing was that he seemed to have forgotten the dreaded Diane and was having a good time, and soon I'd forgotten about her too and I was leaping around the room like one of Wayne Sleep's dancers doing all kinds of things I didn't even know I could do. I hadn't let myself go like that for ages and I don't believe Harry had either. It must have had something to do with the music and the effect we had on each other. Anyway I just danced madly and enjoyed it and after about half an hour we both fell into chairs, exhausted.

'Your face is shiny,' Harry panted, grinning happily.

'And yours is red and sweaty,' I laughed.

When we'd got our breath I helped him push the furniture back into place and we both gratefully downed an iced coke. Harry's depression seemed to have miraculously vanished.

'That was terrific,' he said. 'We must do it again.'

'Smashing.' I glanced at the clock. 'Oh no! Look at the time! I've got to get up at dawn tomorrow.'

He saw me to the lift.

I got in. 'See you er . . . sometime then,' I said.

He gave me a lovely cheesy grin. 'Next time, with luck, you'll be able to meet Diane.'

'Fantastic,' I said.

Yeah . . .

Chapter 7

Ned. As the days rolled by I became increasingly worried about him. Carla was now working three whole days a week so I always took Ned to his nursery school, collected him again and entertained him for the afternoon. She tried to be home in time to bath him and give him his supper but Ned, for some reason, seemed rather off his mother and clung to me. Naturally this distressed Carla although she was quite sensible about it.

As for his father, as soon as the child heard his key in the flat door he fled to his room and refused to come out again. Giles tried everything, smiles and jokes and games, you name it he did it, but Ned was not be won over. No way. Poor old Giles – I actually felt quite sorry for him.

Then Ned had these amazing tantrums. Given the slightest excuse he would suddenly go red in the face and start yelling the house down. His little body would go completely rigid with his arms straight at his sides and his fists tightly clenched and he would roar and roar. It was quite frightening. If we were at home when it happened I'd just sit down with a book and pretend to ignore him, and after a bit he'd calm down but, honestly, it left us both exhausted. If we were out somewhere it was more difficult and I just coped the best way possible at the time.

Of course I knew all along what the trouble was and I think Carla did too but she wasn't ready to discuss it with me. You see Giles and Carla argued and quarrelled all the time and little by little the atmosphere in the flat became unbearable. If I hadn't gone out a lot, either with June and Sven, or Lion, or with one of the nannies I'd met at various kiddies' parties, I couldn't have stood it. As it was I just took cover in my room until the latest row died down.

I'm a pretty uncomplicated sort of person, not much

given to moods or fits of introspection. I can't understand people who mess their lives about but suddenly I seemed to be surrounded by people busy doing just that. Harry upstairs, eating his heart out for this beautiful Diane person; June downstairs, actually hesitating over an operation which would give her a nearly normal life, and Carla and Giles, blessed with a lovely little boy, well paid jobs and a nice home, tearing into each other like a couple of snarling dogs.

My sympathies were, as usual, mainly with Carla. Giles, excitable as a prima donna, was nervy and jumpy and found fault with everything and Carla's good nature was stretched to breaking point. To be honest, their attitudes to life and their temperaments were so different that I often wondered how they'd managed to find enough in common to get married in the first place.

Meanwhile poor little Ned suffered. I suppose I should have plucked up the courage to have it out with them, but I didn't know how to do it without criticizing or being rude.

Anyway I'd decided not to go home for a while because of Frank the butcher so, like it or not, I was stuck with the rowing Robsons.

One Saturday in October Lion had to deliver a new car to a client in Devon and asked me to go with him. We had to make a very early start but he promised to stop at a super hotel for lunch on our way back to London. I'd really have preferred to hang around the flat on the off chance of seeing Harry but I knew that would be kind of stupid. I'd seen him several times since that first occasion, and although he'd obviously been glad of my company – especially when I buckled-to and cleared up the kitchen – his heart and mind were elsewhere (give you one guess!) and he never made a definite date to see me again, but at least we'd become friends.

Anyway on the Friday before Lion and I went to Devon, Giles flew to Scotland for a business conference and Carla and Ned went to stay with her parents in Horsham for the weekend.

As luck would have it, on my way back from the hairdresser's on Friday evening I met Harry going into the apartment block. He was carrying a huge bunch of flowers and radiating a dotty happiness.

'Diane's coming for supper tomorrow,' he burbled merrily.

I glanced at the flowers. 'Then let's hope she puts in an appearance this time.' I suppose I was envious and wanted to puncture his pretty balloon but he was too far gone to take any notice.

When the lift reached our floor I asked if he'd like to come in for a coffee but he shook his head.

'Thanks, but not just now. I'm going to put these flowers in water and then start on my Boeuf Bourguignon. It takes me days to prepare a meal and I must have everything ready for tomorrow.'

Perhaps it was the difference in our upbringing or something but he sometimes sounded so middle-aged!

'Sounds like you're setting the seduction scene,' I joked.

He grinned cockily. 'Maybe I am.'

That threw me a bit I can tell you. 'Well the best of British luck,' I said sarcastically.

Did he notice? Not likely!

'Thanks. Hey – Diane's busy the day after tomorrow so why not come up? You and I can eat the left-overs.'

'Okay.'

The left-overs. That just about described my importance in Harry's life.

The chill of approaching winter was in the air when Lion called for me at 6 a.m. and I was glad of my new suede boots, brown cords and the thick yellow sweater Gran had knitted for me before she died.

'Hey kid, you look like a canary on stilts,' Lion said whisking round to open the passenger door. I think he meant it as a compliment to my long legs.

He looked pretty smart himself in a sporty checked jacket and twill trousers. He'd even had his hair cut in quite a trendy way but then I suppose he had to clean up his image before setting off in the fabulous blue Mercedes!

'How long until we get there?' I asked.

'Depends on the traffic. Three hours – something like that.'

Soon we were heading for the motorway and Lion turned on the radio.

'Hope you don't mind. I'm kind of used to the noise. I find it relaxing.'

I didn't mind. Far from it. Lion and I didn't have that much to talk about at the best of times. Three hours unadulterated chat might put a big strain on our relationship. As it was I just lay back luxuriating in the comfort of the car, and finished my night's sleep.

I came-to hours later, on the outskirts of Exeter.

'Enjoyed the trip?' Lion asked with the merest hint of sarcasm.

I laughed. 'Sorry. I always sleep in cars and trains. What's new?'

'We are heading for the country mansion of Mrs

McGilvray-Barnfeather so I hope you've been practising your curtsey.'

'You bet.'

We came to a long drive, bordered by poplar trees and arrived at a huge grey stone house with dozens of long windows. It all looked rather intimidating.

However, as it turned out I didn't have to drop my curtsey to Mrs McGilvray-B because the only person we saw was her chauffeur!

Lion quickly did his business and then came to meet me in the study where I'd been looking at the enormous collection of beautifully bound leather books.

'Mission complete pardner. We're free to go. What would you like to do?'

'Can we go to the sea?'

'Sure.'

'Oh Lion that would be amazing! I'd love a swim.'

He looked slightly stunned. 'But it's almost winter.'

'Yeah I know it's crazy but I just feel like it.'

He shook his head wonderingly. 'God, what it is to be young!'

Having arrived in a Merc we departed in an equally immaculate BMW. In fact it gleamed even more brightly than the new car.

'I've got a customer anxiously waiting for this little lady,' Lion said smugly as we sped down the tree-lined drive.

The sea made me feel alive, hurling itself about in a wild, abandoned manner while streaky clouds chased each other across the blue sky and seagulls screeched piercingly as they circled the bay.

It was too rough to swim so I took off my boots and rolled up my cords and ran about playing ducks and drakes and combing the beach for shells.

'Oh Lion isn't this great?' I shouted, dashing backwards to escape the spray as the waves crashed on to the shore.

He nodded but I don't think he was having that much fun because he was just standing there with his hands thrust into his pockets, staring at me with this kind of puzzled look as if to say, 'What am I doing here with this mad woman?'

Suddenly I felt I wasn't being fair to him. After all he'd invited me to come so it was up to me to see that he enjoyed it too. Going up to him I slid my hand into the crook of his elbow.

'Thank you for bringing me,' I said shyly.

He put his arms around me and I put mine around him, then he kissed me, not like the other times when I'd had to fight him off but gently, almost tenderly. His lips were cold but his tongue was warm and we stood there for a long while, mouth to mouth, while the wind whipped our hair about and the gulls shrieked overhead and the sea crashed in our ears.

I think I'll always remember that kiss.

But the combination of wind and sea and kissing make a person hungry and I was glad to get into the car again and head for lunch.

'I know the couple who run this joint,' Lion said as we parked in front of a pretty hotel on the outskirts of Exeter. 'Jan used to be a model and Nick was an airline pilot. They mortgaged their souls to buy this place three years ago. It's a great hideaway for a dirty weekend. Of course I'm not suggesting anything.'

'Never thought you were.'

He put his hand on my leg. 'I will one day though.'

I grinned and shook it off. 'Is that a threat or a promise?'

We went straight into the bar where Jan, a lanky brunette, fell on Lion's neck with cries of joy, and when all that was over Lion ordered a coke for me and a Pimms for himself. I'd learned my lesson about trusting him to decide my drinks!

I was fully expecting to feel put down by this Jan person because she was so jet-setish in her silky shirt with a slender gold chain disappearing down her tanned cleavage – you know the sort of thing. But I was wrong. She was vcry friendly and interested, especially when I told her about our pub. Then several other people came into the bar and she had to attend to them.

While Lion got stuck into his Pimms I sat back and examined my surroundings. Because of my background, hotels had always fascinated me and this one was particularly elegant. The bar looked like a sitting room in a private house. A log fire burned in the grate and there were plenty of comfortable armchairs, and attractive knick-knacks everywhere.

'Don't these things ever get nicked?' I asked Lion.

He shrugged. 'Sure, but Jan likes it this way, even if she does lose the odd piece from time to time.'

'Golly. They even nick the beer mats at home. You'd be amazed.'

Lion shook his head. 'Not me kid. You're talking to a veteran. I grew up on the rough side of Portsmouth. Most of our neighbours did a stretch for something or other. My dad was a docker and my mum charred in the old Pig and Whistle for years. It's gone now. There's a block of fancy offices there instead.'

'I thought you grew up in the States,' I said. 'You use so much American jargon.'

'That's because I lived at the movies. Clint Eastwood was my idol.'

Clint Eastwood. Would you believe it? The things you learn about people you think you know quite well!

The crowded dining-room looked over the garden and we were given a table in a recess near the bay window in which stood a table set for two. Jan came over to take our lunch order, and then sped off in the direction of the kitchen. I was really looking forward to my avocado with prawns and was just about to say so to Lion when I noticed a good-looking couple pass our table, and take their places at the table in the window.

The woman facing me had one of those hard executive-type faces, all sticky-out bones and glossy lips. She had short, dark, neatly cut hair and wore a cream trouser suit with an angora sweater and a rope of pearls. I know I haven't described her very well because, quite honestly, I was in a state of total shock. You see the man sitting with his back to me was Giles Robson and he was supposed to be in Scotland.

Chapter 8

Although I caught the woman's eye I had the sense immediately, and casually, to look away again. It's odd but when something as unexpected as that occurs it seems to take ages to sink in. I remember registering Giles's presence, his sculpted fair head, the new Italian jacket he was so pleased with, the particular way he sat at table – leaning slightly forward to enhance his integrity and charm, then my mind went blank. It couldn't be Giles because he'd flown to Scotland yesterday evening. But here he was. And with a very chic looking lady too.

All this passed through my brain in slow motion while I looked calmly beyond the couple into the garden. The wind was busy tearing the leaves from the trees and blowing them across the neat lawn. Winter's nearly here I thought . . .

When panic struck it was like the blow of an axe. Stunning. I had to get out before he saw me. Without saying anything to Lion I got up from the table, walked swiftly out of the dining-room and made straight for the 'Ladies' where I cooled my sweaty face under the tap and considered my position. Could Giles possibly be enjoying a legit business lunch. On a Saturday? Frankly it didn't look like it. Not considering the adoring way she was gazing at him across the table. Perhaps he hadn't gone to Scotland at all but had driven down straight from London. Oh poor Carla! On the other hand I must be very careful not to jump to conclusions. Somehow I had to check the facts and get Lion away before Giles saw me. But how?

I washed my hands, yanked my sweater down over my hips and, keeping a wary eye on the dining-room door, I made for the bar. Jan was alone and looked surprised when she saw me.

'Hallo. I thought you and Lion were having lunch.'

I glanced uneasily around as if expecting Giles to materialize at my elbow. 'We are. Well, we were but I'm not feeling that good so I thought I'd come out for a breather.'

'Oh dear. I am sorry. What's the trouble?' She looked so genuinely concerned that I felt a bit of a heel at having to lie.

'I'm er . . . feeling a bit sick. I expect it's nothing but I don't feel like eating. Could I sip a little soda water please?'

'Of course.' She poured some into a glass and passed it across the bar. 'Do you want me to fetch Lion?'

'Yeah, if I don't feel better soon.'

She nodded sympathetically and got on with clearing up: polishing the counter and emptying the ashtrays – all the chores I knew so well.

'I think I recognize someone in the dining-room,' I said casually. 'The man in the window. Fair. Quite good looking. Is he on telly or something?'

Jan laughed. 'He'd be flattered to hear you thought that.'

'Funny, I could have sworn . . . '

'No, that's Geoffrey Roebuck, one of our regulars. Likes to get away from it all I suppose. I think he's something in the city.'

'Mrs Roebuck's rather gorgeous isn't she?'

Jan gave a perfectly clean ashtray an elaborate rub down. 'Mm, she is.'

'I bet she likes to get away from it now and then too. Especially with a smashing husband like that.'

She didn't answer and I wondered if I'd gone too far, then she smiled pleasantly. 'How are you feeling now?'

'Awful. Please could you fetch Lion?' I wouldn't get any more out of her and it was time to get out of there.

When Lion appeared he looked half concerned and half annoyed. 'What's all this crap about you feeling ill? You were okay twenty minutes ago.'

I lolled against the wall trying to look bad. 'Yeah I

know. Look I'm sorry Lion but could we go home?'

'Can't you wait until I've finished lunch?'

'No. I think I'm getting something nasty. I'd like to go now please.'

He turned to Jan. 'Sorry about lunch sweetheart. I'll pay for it of course.'

She patted his arm reassuringly. 'Nonsense. These things happen. No bones broken. Look forward to seeing you the next time you're in the area.'

We said goodbye and went through to the foyer. Lion disappeared into the 'Gents' and I found myself alone by the desk, looking down at the open hotel register.

The drive back to London was painfully silent. You couldn't blame Lion; I'd ruined his day, but I now wanted to put as much mileage as possible between Giles and me before going into lengthy explanations.

When things go wrong I often find myself taking refuge in sleep and no sooner had we left Exeter behind than I nodded off again. When I awoke we were zooming smoothly along the 303 towards London.

'Feeling better?' Lion asked when I sat up.

'Yeah much. I wrecked your day didn't I? I'm sorry. Really I am.'

'You certainly did. What was it all about? You were no more feeling sick than I was.'

'How do you know?'

'Your colour was too good, and you were suspiciously keen to get away.'

I shrugged, slightly annoyed that he'd seen through my act. 'Oh well, over to you Miss Marple.'

'No come on Matty. I think you owe me an explanation.'

I sighed. 'Okay. Remember that couple sitting at the table in the window?'

'Sure.'

'Well, the man was my employer Giles Robson. He is supposed to be in Scotland on business. Jan said they go there quite a lot.'

'So what? Perhaps the steely-jawed lady is his cousin or something.'

'Huh! When you were in the loo I looked through the register. They'd signed in as Geoffrey Roebuck and Gemma Pascoe. Not even Mr and Mrs! I checked with Jan – although she didn't know what I was doing.'

'I see.' We must have gone half a mile when he suddenly began to laugh and he went on and on as though he'd never stop.

I didn't. I was furious. I mean how unfeeling can you get? There were poor Carla and little Ned spending an innocent weekend with her parents while her rotten hubby was cheating on her with a glossy female tycoon in Devon. It wasn't fair, and I said so.

Lion wiped his eyes and tucked away his hanky. 'You'd better give up the idea that life is fair right now. It's not. It never has been and never will be. Anyway you and your randy employer have given me a good laugh so you are forgiven – provided you agree to cook me a decent supper.'

Well, honestly, I felt it was the least I could do.

By the time we reached London it was raining. Lion parked the car and we made a short dash through the downpour into the building. Once in the flat we dried out and Lion switched on the telly while I investigated the contents of the fridge. I found the remains of a cooked chicken and some reasonable vegetables and decided to stir-fry them. I was starving. At least Lion had managed to enjoy his avocado before I dragged him away!

While I cooked I thought. And I thought. Should I tell Carla about seeing Giles with this other woman? If he were having an affair he would probably be feeling hellishly guilty which might explain his impossible behaviour at home. On the other hand what good would it do to tell her? Perhaps if I kept quiet it would soon fizzle out and things would go on as before – with Carla none the wiser. It was all very difficult.

Outside the rain kept up a steady deluge but inside it was really quite cosy. I changed into my cherry track suit and slipper socks; Lion took off his jacket and rolled up his shirt sleeves and we settled down to eat in front of the telly.

It wasn't until I'd stacked the dishes in the sink and plonked myself wearily down on the living-room sofa that the trouble started. I don't have to tell you what the trouble was. Yeah, sex.

Lion suddenly leaned over, grabbed me and began kissing me. Okay – so far as it went, but it didn't stop there. First he got his hand up my top and started groping and no sooner had I dealt with that than he climbed on top of me and began to kiss me passionately.

When you're in that situation it's no good murmuring 'Was that the phone?' or, 'Wait while I tie my shoe-lace', because when a fella knows what he wants, that's what he goes all out to get. You have to make a lightning decision – i.e. will you or won't you? Well, I made it pretty quickly and I was trying to get it across as tactfully as possible when the door bell rang.

I heaved a sigh of relief but Lion dragged himself crossly to a sitting position.

'Who the hell can that be at this time of night?'

'It's only nine o'clock,' I said brightly, heading for the door.

When I opened it who should be there but Harry. Behind him stood a girl.

'Er . . . hallo Matty,' he said. 'Hope you don't mind us calling but Diane's in a bit of a fix.'

'Come in,' I said. 'Great to see you both.'

I closed the door and we all stood awkwardly in the Robson's dim hallway. I hoped I didn't look as if I'd just been fighting off a sex maniac. The girl leant against the book shelves, hands thrust in the pockets of her dark skirt, her crimson shirt open at the throat exposing yards of cleavage one way and a swan-like neck the other.

'Diane's got something to ask you,' Harry said. I thought he seemed a bit embarrassed.

I waited politely.

'Tampons,' she said baldly. 'The need is somewhat urgent.'

I nodded. 'Okay, follow me. Harry why don't you go into the sitting-room. You'll find Lion there. I don't think you've met.'

'Thanks Matty.' He gave me a grateful smile and sloped off.

I took Diane to my room and gave her the necessary. 'Bathroom's across the corridor,' I said.

'Thanks.' She didn't seem in any hurry to depart. In fact she had a good look around, taking in the photographs of Mum and Dad, my old teddy bear, and all my stuff lying everywhere. Then she began smoothing her hair in front of my mirror. I sat on the bed and let her get on with it.

I'd like to say she looked like the back end of a bus

but unfortunately she didn't. She looked fabulous. Her copper head gleamed like it had been polished or something. Her peachy skin glowed, and her enormous green eyes sparkled with self-interest. Her figure was the kind poets rave about – perky boobs, long back, small waist and hips, slender legs and perfect ankles. I could have killed her.

'It must be great to be an actress,' I said. I mean she was just standing there adoring herself and I had to say something to wake her up.

My question brought her out of her reverie. 'What? Oh yeah. It's okay. Better than being a nanny I guess.'

I could feel my hackles rising. 'I'm not exactly a nanny.'

She raised her delicate eyebrows. 'I thought you looked after a kid.'

'I do but I do lots of other things as well.'

'Such as?'

'Oh . . . cooking and that.'

'Ugh!' She made a yukky face. 'I hate cooking and housework.'

'Perhaps you'll never need to do it,' I said cheerfully, determined not to let her see how she was riling me.

She laughed and strolled to the door. 'I'll bloody well see that I don't!'

I heard the bathroom lock click then I opened the window to let in some much-needed fresh air, and went along to the sitting room.

Lion had recovered his humour and was gassing away merrily to Harry. They were deeply absorbed in the merits of the BMW versus those of the Audi, so I left them to it and went off to make coffee. When I returned Diane was back, stretched out languidly in an armchair as if she owned the place. Lion couldn't take his eyes off her and Diane, fully aware of the impression she was making kept gazing at him through semi-closed lids and blowing cigarette smoke in his direction.

'I'd like a Mercedes drop-head,' she said. (We were still on cars.)

Lion saw his chance. 'I could probably let you test-drive one.'

She laughed. 'You don't really think I could afford one do you?'

'Even so . . . '

'Really?' She looked at him with renewed interest.

'Sure.' He extracted a small diary from his jacket pocket. 'Let's see. How about next Thursday at twelve? We could have lunch somewhere afterwards.'

'Okay. Why not? I'll give you a ring when I've checked my dates.'

'You're on. Here's my business card.'

During this conversation I could see Harry getting glummer and glummer but of course he couldn't say anything. I had a feeling this wasn't the first time he had seen Diane in full siren form, luring men to the death of the heart, so to speak. I felt really sorry for him. Trying to bring him into the limelight, I said,

'Did Harry cook you a brilliant dinner Diane? I saw the ingredients going up in the lift – real gourmet stuff.'

She smothered a tiny yawn. 'Oh yeah, it was great – if you like that sort of thing. Actually I'm into vegetarian cooking now.'

'You didn't tell me,' Harry protested mildly.

'Didn't I? Oh well . . . ' She offered him a vague, sweet smile.

'So you're an actress,' Lion said. 'When are we going to see you on telly?'

As a matter of fact I've got an interview with someone on Monday,' she said, sparkling away at him. 'At the moment I'm still at drama school but if I get a good offer I probably won't stay the course. A lot of it is very boring. I want to get out and start work.'

'But won't you find it difficult to get an Equity card?' I asked.

She looked surprised that I was still there. 'I expect someone will fix it for me, they usually do.'

I bet they do, I thought nastily!

Diane stretched luxuriously. 'Well . . . this has been a great evening but I must go home and get my beauty sleep.'

Harry jumped up with alacrity. 'I'll ring for a taxi.'

'Dear Harry.' She might have been patting a small dog on the head.

Lion reached for his jacket. 'My car's outside,' he said casually. 'I'll give you a lift if you like.'

She rewarded him with a dazzling neon-smile. 'You're sure it's no trouble?'

'I'm going now anyway so I may as well drop you off.'

I glanced at Harry's face. He was suffering, I mean really suffering. It must be awful to be in love like that.

'Does she live with her parents?' I asked when they'd gone.

He shook his head miserably. 'No she's got her own flat. I only hope he gets her there safely.'

'Oh he'll make sure of that,' I said lightly.

He nodded, looking even more miserable. 'I suppose so.'

If I'd fondly imagined – and I honestly think I had – that once Diane had proved faithless he'd immediately turn to me, I couldn't have been more wrong.

Muttering a belated 'Thanks for your help Matty', he drifted out of the door and into the waiting lift without a backward glance.

Never mind, I thought, my turn will come!

Chapter 9

Although I went out like a light as soon as my head touched the pillow I didn't sleep well. Nightmare after nightmare chased me through the small hours. One was particularly vivid. I was sitting at the same table Lion and I had occupied at lunch. A man came and sat at the table in the window. The place opposite him was empty. Naturally I assumed it was Giles but when he turned around it was Ned and as I looked beyond him out of the window I was horrified to see a towering wave rushing towards us from the garden. Just as it was about to break I woke up.

I awoke, for good, very early in the morning, my brain in a whirl. Should I or shouldn't I tell Carla about Giles? How long would it be before she discovered the truth for herself? And what then? Separation? Divorce? No wonder I'd had nightmares about poor Ned.

The weekend in the country seemed to have done Carla good because she left for work on Monday in better spirits than usual. Ned, however, was very truculent. In fact he behaved so roughly at Joanna's birthday party that afternoon that I felt quite ashamed. I know that sounds ridiculous. I mean how can you be ashamed of a four-year-old child? But when he stamped all over little Joanna's presents, then started throwing peanut butter sandwiches at the other kids and creating general havoc, I muttered an excuse about having to get home early and took him away.

I was pretty tight-lipped I can tell you, and it wasn't until we were on the bus that I felt calm enough to speak.

'What got into you then?'

He looked up, all innocence. 'What do you mean?'

'Chucking food about like that. What's Mummy going to say?'

He shrugged and pressed his nose against the window.

'Okay. What will Daddy say then?'

'You won't tell Daddy,' he said confidently.

'Won't I? Why not?'

'Because you're afraid of him.'

I laughed – or tried to.

'You are,' he insisted. 'Mummy is too. So am I.' He breathed on the glass and began drawing patterns on the steamy surface.

'Daddy wouldn't hurt you,' I said. 'He loves you.' But he didn't reply.

When we got off the bus he seemed okay, quite cheerful in fact as he skipped along chatting about this and that. One thing about Ned, he was amazingly attractive. He had curly flaxen hair and enormous blue eyes and Carla always dressed him in primary colours so that he stood out in the dull London streets like a child in one of his story books. Of course people always thought I was his mother and we were often stopped in shops by doting old women. Ned was used to having his hair stroked and being chucked under the chin. He was very good about it really.

Anyway, as I said, he was sweet and cheerful on the walk home and it wasn't until I was putting the key into the lock of the apartment block that I realized why. Grabbing my wrist he stopped me going through the open door.

'You won't tell Daddy will you?' he begged, his eyes wider and bluer than the summer skies.

'Not this time,' I said severely. 'But if you do it again . . . '

'Oh I won't Matty. I won't really.'

Poor little tyke. My heart bled for him.

After putting Ned to bed I had a bath and washed my hair. I must say I rather like myself all pink and steamy, after a hot bath. I look a bit like that painting of Venus bobbing about on a shell in the sea. I know it sounds a bit vain but I expect lots of us are vain when no one else is around. Anyway, after admiring myself for a while I dressed in my pink cords and silver-grey sweater, made up my eyes and held the usual debate about whether or not to wear lipstick.

Lipstick is always a problem. If I wear a bright one I tend to look a bit tarty. On the other hand sometimes you want to look, well, sensual don't you? After all I had to compete with the devastating Diane. So I put on Pink Flamingo followed by a natural gloss and there I was, all eyes and mouth and a mass of springy hair held to one side with a pink plastic clip.

All this, mind you, just to be allowed to gobble up Diane's left-overs!

Harry took ages answering the door. When he finally opened it he looked so down in the dumps that I wondered if he'd had bad news or something,

'Oh it's you Matty.'

'Yeah. Weren't you expecting me?'

He scratched his left ear. 'Was I?'

'You said to come and polish off the left-overs.'

'Did I?' He still didn't invite me in.

'Never mind,' I said briskly. 'You've obviously forgotten. It doesn't matter.' And turning away I made for the stairs.

He ran after me and grabbed my arm. 'It does matter. I'm sorry Matty. Do come in. Really. There's a ton of stuff in the fridge. I made far too much.'

'But you obviously want to be alone.'

'That's the last thing I want,' he said practically dragging me back to the flat.

It was a tricky situation. Of course I knew what was bugging the guy. His precious Diane had gone home with Lion, and Harry had spent hours imagining what they'd been up to. I didn't have to imagine – I was sure! Not that it mattered to me anyway – apart from a natural twinge of hurt pride. In fact, so far as Harry was concerned, it suited me down to the ground. However, I thought it best to keep off the subject and while he gloomily fixed us a beer each, I resurrected the Boeuf Bourguignon, prepared pommes gratinées and sprouts with walnuts and poured out my problem about Giles and the other woman.

Harry sat on the edge of the kitchen table and listened. He was a great listener. He looked at you all the time and kept very still so you knew that he was paying attention, and by the time I'd finished the story he looked much brighter. I suppose it does everyone good to listen to other people's worries for a change.

'You can't tell Carla,' he said. 'That would be playing God. It was just bad luck that you landed up in the same hotel.'

'But I hate having to deceive her,' I wailed. 'I feel so rotten knowing about her two-timing husband.'

'It's none of your business,' he insisted. 'Just forget the whole thing.'

I sighed. 'It's so difficult. I want to bop Giles on the nose every time I see him.'

'Well don't. He might bop you back.' He gave me one of his gentle smiles. 'You're a funny girl. You really care about people don't you? Look at you now – getting supper for me when I should be getting it for you.'

'I'm enjoying it.'

He shook his head in a bemused manner. 'Can't think why. I'm not very good company at the moment.'

He looked so dismal that I longed to tell him to stop wasting his emotions on Diane. I mean, couldn't he see what she was like? Selfish, vain and spoilt. No good saying anything though; it would be like telling a junkie he didn't need his next fix.

So I went on cooking (I'd decided to add onion soup to the menu) and while I cried over the onions I trotted out a couple of my Mum's ancient music-hall type jokes, hoping to cheer him up. It did too because he laughed and said,

'It's nice to have a girl around the place.'

'Doing the chores and that?'

'No. I don't care about the chores. They only get done when I feel like it.'

'All right for some. Others have to work for a living.'

'I work too you know. Matter of fact I find studying a real grind and I've got years of it ahead of me.'

'Can't say I envy you.'

'No, you don't seem the academic type.' He cocked his head to one side and looked me over thoughtfully. 'But you don't seem the nanny type either.'

I peeked into the oven to check on the beef. 'What is the nanny type? Wait!' I closed the oven door. 'I'll answer that for you. There isn't one. Nannies these days are all types: bright, dim; pretty, plain; good, bad. I mean the Princess of Wales was a nanny once wasn't she?'

'Okay, you've made your point. So you're a career nanny?'

'I never said that.'

'Come on Matty! You fell into this job accidently – you told me all about it. You're no more a nanny than I am. Ned's a nice little boy but he'll be off to school soon and what then? Another nice little boy? One of Carla Robson's friends' children perhaps? You'll have to think about it sometime you know.'

'Something will turn up.' I said cheerfully although, to be honest, I didn't relish the thought of being passed around the Kensington and Chelsea nurseries like some sort of faithful old dog.

'Matty? Oh yes I've finished with her so you can have her next. Feed her well and she'll do anything for you.' Hmm. I'd met a few of those and the older they got the more pathetic they were.

'What do you really enjoy?' Harry asked. 'I mean what did you dream about doing before you left school?'

'Nothing really. I never thought a lot about it. There was always too much going on. But since you ask, I enjoy lots of things.'

'Such as?'

'Well . . . ' I sniffed the soup appreciatively. 'Cooking for one.'

'Enough to make a career out of it?'

I laughed. 'Who'd be rash enough to let me loose in their kitchen every day? My gran taught me to cook but I haven't any qualifications.'

'You could get some. In fact you could take a catering course.'

'What, go back to school?'

'Not school exactly. College. It's very different.'

I shook my head. 'Dad would never wear it. He'd think it was just another passing phase.'

'Have you had lots of passing phases?'

'Some. I've been thrown out of a couple of jobs too. Once for giving a little kid a bright red hair dye and once for telling the owner of a restaurant that she was a liar and a cheat.'

Harry threw back his head and laughed. It was lovely – a genuine bubble of mirth exploding like a fire-cracker in the dark little kitchen.

'Oh Matty, you are worth your weight in gold! Specially when one is feeling down.'

'Yeah, I'm all things bright and beautiful,' I joked wryly. It's a bit disconcerting to have the knack of tickling everyone's funny bone when you are longing to be avidly lusted after.

Then, as if he'd read my thoughts, he said, 'As a matter of fact you're looking particularly pretty this evening too.'

Funny and pretty! Things were looking up, and by the time we picked up our drinks and left the kitchen for a while, you could say I was both hungry and hopeful. To crown my mood, Harry even draped his arm casually around my shoulders, and my stomach flipped over.

We strolled into the unlit drawing-room and crossed over to the french-windows. Outside it was still raining and we had a bird's-eye view of domed umbrellas and their nimble-footed owners dodging the puddles.

For a while we stood still, not speaking, but Harry's arm felt tense across my back and I knew we were working up to something. I say we, because I was pretty tense too. Something I'd day-dreamed about was within an ace of happening but there's many a slip . . .

'On a night just like this I remember rescuing a girl from the jaws of death by exposure to the elements,' Harry said, 'only I don't remember reaping the just reward.'

I stared out at the rain, my heart going like the clappers. 'What reward?'

'Oh there's always a reward.'

'First I've heard of it.'

'Then you're not very well up with your fairy stories. By rights I should extract a passionate kiss from her.' His hand crept to the back of my head and he gently turned my face to his. Behind him the Lord ancestral portraits gleamed in the street-light – proud noses, beady eyes, sensual mouths . . . I moved closer; his free arm enfolded me, his warm breath fanned my cheek, our lips met . . . I sighed deeply . . . Suddenly the telephone shrilled and we both nearly leapt out of our skins.

Harry crossed the room in a couple of strides.

'Yes? . . . Diane! Where are you? . . .What on earth are you doing there? . . . You mean he hasn't turned up? Well of all the rotten . . . ! What are you going to do now? . . . Well I suppose I could but someone's here at the moment . . . Okay, okay. I'll have to find a taxi – always tricky on a wet night so I might be some time. What's your number in case I need to call you?'

He jotted it down on the edge of a newspaper. I watched, joy turned to ashes. He put down the receiver.

'That was Diane.' At least he had the grace to look guilty.

'Yeah?'

'She'd arranged to meet some guy from the Beeb at a club in Hampstead but he stood her up.'

'So?' I wasn't about to make this easy for him.

'Well she's really miserable and hasn't enough money for a taxi so I'd better go and get her.'

'Why can't she take a bus?'

'It's her new shoes. They hurt. And she hasn't got a rain coat or anything.'

I guffawed rudely. 'You're really going to let her pull that one?'

'It's raining cats and dogs. Diane hates rain.'

'Spoils her make-up does it?'

'Don't be mean Matty. It's not like you.'

I folded my arms obstinately. 'It's just that I hate to see you running around after her all the time.'

'That's ridiculous. I don't.'

'You do.'

But I could tell it was water off a duck's back. He wasn't even listening. Instead he was going through his pockets to see how much money he had, then he made straight for the cupboard in the hall and stuffed himself into a rain coat – all in the space of about three minutes.

I watched disconsolately. 'What about supper?'

'Supper?' He hesitated, his hand on the front door knob. 'Oh yes. You must stay and eat it of course. Turn on the telly or something.'

'Gee thanks!'

The sarcasm penetrated his love-sick brain and suddenly he seemed to realize what he was doing. Releasing the door knob he came back to me and put his hands on my shoulders.

'Matty, I know this is a rotten way to treat you but what am I to do? She's miserable and stranded in bloody Hampstead. I must go and rescue her.' He gave a wry little laugh. 'That seems to be my role in life!'

'I thought so many people were dying to help her,' I said sulkily. 'That's the impression she gives anyway.'

He smiled knowingly, the man with the inside knowledge. 'That's all talk. She's very vulnerable really.'

About as vulnerable as a baracuda, I thought bitterly.

I stood in the doorway and watched him disappear into the lift then I went back into the kitchen. I felt like throwing the onion soup and everything straight into the bin, but food is food and with half the world starving you do think twice about things like that, so I ate it. All of it. Harry's portion and mine. Then I spotted a delicious Ogen melon sitting in solitary state on the fruit dish and I chomped my way through that too. After that I discovered a bottle of Creme de Menthe in a kitchen cupboard, and pouring some into a cup I sipped it while I did the washing up. Then I had some more. After all I had been invited to supper.

Things had been going so well too.

Just my lousy luck again!

Chapter 10

Now I'm not the sort who gets easily depressed but after that non-evening with Harry I did feel a bit low. I mean what can you do with a guy who simply won't face things? Diane was using him – anyone could see that – but you could have told him a million times and he'd have denied it and gone on being a door-mat.

I often wondered why she bothered with him; he just didn't seem her type. Diane would be in her element surrounded by hooray-henrys with Daddys in Lloyds and Mummys who dabbled in interior design. But I don't suppose hooray-henrys are all that reliable – not, as you might say, over willing to turn out on a rainy night and collect a girl by taxi from an address miles away in Hampstead. Then of course she'd go for Harry's background – his diplomat father, the well polished antiques, the portrait of his great-granny in court-gear. All that snob stuff would immensely appeal to her. But after she'd known him for a while she probably got bored with his quiet, excessive devotion. I'd seen the wild man in Harry when we'd danced like mad things in his drawing room but maybe he'd never done anything like that with her. Perhaps he was so besotted that all he could do was moon around trying to please her. I just bet he'd never kissed her like he kissed me before she managed to kill it with her wretched phone call. She might have had more respect for him if he had.

All through the next week I spent hours turning things over in my mind. Sometimes I was tempted to chuck the idea of Harry and me altogether. I'd certainly proved that he was attracted to me but what was the good of that when, at a crook of Diane's little finger he was off to lick her dainty boots? On the other hand I instinctively felt I should hang around a bit longer. I mean he could be fun when he wasn't thinking about her. And he had really beautiful eyes and such a come-on grin.

But I'd have made a lousy actress and it was really hard for me to lay on the old pal routine while hopefully waiting for him to get wise to Diane.

Anyway I couldn't bring myself to visit Harry for a while, and June seemed to be out a lot, and Lion didn't ring (well we all know why, don't we?) so I spent my free time lounging around the flat painting my nails or commiserating with other nannies about their love-lives, their unruly charges and inconsiderate employers. Then one Saturday morning – believe it or not Giles was away AGAIN – I wandered into the kitchen to make coffee and toast and found Carla sitting disconsolately at the table, a bottle of whiskey and a glass in front of her. At ten in the morning! I could hear Ned's trains chuffing around the play-room next door. Today, thank heavens, he was his mother's responsibility. Carla looked up as I came in.

'Morning Matty. Do you know what day it is?'

I yawned. 'You're at home so it must be Saturday. It could be Sunday but I haven't heard any church bells.'

'Great thinking. It's not only Saturday. It's my birthday.' She poured herself a tot of whiskey and downed it in one. 'Cheers!'

'Oh Carla! And I didn't even give you a card.'

She looked disappointed. 'You're not the only one.'

'You mean Giles didn't . . . ?'

'Nope.'

'Gosh, if I'd known Ned and I would have done something special.'

'Yes well, thanks anyway. I suppose I'm feeling a bit sorry for myself. Thirty is quite a milestone in a girl's life, it shouldn't go unmarked.'

'Right.' I dropped the bread into the toaster feeling awful. I'd been so preoccupied with my own life lately that I hadn't given much thought to Carla's problems. Now they all rushed back and for the umpteenth time I silently cursed Giles for being such a complete and utter turd.

I took my coffee and sat down at the table, racking my brains for something to cheer her up.

'Let's celebrate,' I said, not very helpfully.

She smiled wistfully. 'Good idea but how? Ned's got another cold so we can't go out. Anyway it's not that long until Christmas and everywhere is so crowded.' Suddenly she sat up, her eyes sparkling. 'I know. Let's give a dinner party.'

'Another one? Who for this time?'

'You of course.'

'Me?' I squeaked.

'Why not? You like giving dinner parties don't you?'

'Dunno. I've never done it.'

'Well now's your chance. We'll have fun getting the food together.' She bounced up and down on her chair, revitalized by the thought of my dinner party.

I shook my head doubtfully. 'I really don't know. I mean who would I ask?'

Carla grabbed a pencil and paper and began writing. 'Well for starters there's that girl downstairs – the one with the crippled foot – and her smashing boyfriend.'

'Sven. You mean June and Sven?'

'Right. Then there's that ginger headed Casanova who drives you around in all those smart cars. Surely you want him?'

'Lion? Yeah well, he's probably doing something else tonight.' (Like making it with Diane!)

'You'd be amazed at how quickly people cancel their engagements when there's a meal and a bottle of decent wine on offer.'

'I could try him I suppose.'

'Good. Now who else shall we ask? What about that boy upstairs – Harry Lord? You know him don't you?'

'Yeah but . . . '

'Come on Matty don't be faint-hearted. Why not ring around now?'

I looked at Carla's beautiful, moon-like face. Her dark eyes were glowing with enthusiasm. I'd wanted her to cheer her up and now I couldn't spoil things by refusing to co-operate.

'Okay,' I said quickly. 'Here goes.'

The long and short of it was that everyone accepted. The only fly in the ointment was Diane. Harry asked if he could bring her as she was coming round to report on her interview with the man from the Beeb. Naturally I agreed, having no choice in the matter.

Then we stuck Ned in front of a lengthy children's video while we got on with preparing the meal. Before we even began I had to nip out and buy all the fresh ingredients. Carla, bless her, paid for everything and I prayed that Giles would never find out – especially when she took his last three bottles of Puligny Montrachet 1976 off the wine rack and put them to cool in the fridge.

Anyway by the time I got back from the shops Carla

had defrosted the puff pastry for the savoury milles-feuilles and I got busy with the smoked trout and sour cream.

'There'll be seven of us,' I said.

Carla carefully laid her strips of pastry aside. 'No six. You and Lion, Harry and Diane and June and Sven.'

'What about you?'

'I'll be too busy waiting on you all to sit down.'

I looked up, shocked. 'Carla you can't!'

'Why on earth not?'

'Because, well, I mean you are my boss.'

She laughed. I loved Carla's laugh. It was deep and rich and genuine. 'Don't look so stricken Matty. I'm looking forward to it.'

She was really beginning to enjoy herself and I must say, so was I. While she prepared the apricot stuffing for the chicken breasts I carefully layered the milles-feuilles.

'Who taught you to cook Matty?' she asked. 'You really seem to know what you are doing.'

'My gran,' I said proudly. 'She was Lady Cowie's cook for years. Actually, she was quite famous. All the guests tried to bribe her to leave Lady Cowie and work for them. She really missed all the fun when she retired to have Mum!

'Did your mum inherit her talent?'

I laughed. 'No way. When Mum left school she and a school friend put together a comic song and dance act and played the clubs for a couple of years before she met Dad. Mum can rustle up a good plain meal but that's about it.'

'Did you ever think of going professional like your

gran? Perhaps running your own restaurant or something?'

Shades of Mrs Dewberry – my erstwhile employer – and her country-style restaurant flashed before my mind's eye. 'No. But I think I know how *not* to run one.'

'I thought about doing it once,' Carla said dreamily. 'I was going to have this delicious, atmospheric little place in a leafy part of London. It would be distinctly plushy and have naughty little alcoves with curtains. Very Edwardian.' She laughed. 'I thought it would probably be filled with randy husbands clandestinely dining their secretaries.'

I looked at her closely. Should I say anything? If so, now was the moment. But what would she gain by losing her peace of mind? No, Harry was right: I must just try and forget what I knew, for Carla's sake.

'Why didn't you go ahead?' I asked.

'Oh a million reasons.' She held up a chicken breast. 'Shall I wrap these in bacon?'

'Yeah, good idea. What reasons Carla? I mean I'm really interested.'

'Okay, but I'll have to use streaky because there isn't any back. My reasons? Well I hadn't any qualifications, experience or money. Three of the best reasons I'd say. Also I had a perfectly good job in advertising. Then, quite soon I met Giles.'

'And you fell for him right away?'

'Yes. He was so . . . so, I don't know, beautiful I suppose.'

I could just imagine it. Lovely Carla, lusciously endowed, like some massive tropical flower, must have been a stunning contrast to the angular, self-centred chicks that inhabit Giles's media world. It was probably an instant knock-out for him too. He must have thought he'd accidently wandered into Heaven.

'Did he ask you to marry him soon?'

'Yes. I was astonished.'

'I'm not,' I said shortly. I mean Giles was no slouch when it came to looking after number one.

We worked in silence for a bit. While Carla was still filling the chicken breasts I got on with the veg. I don't really approve of preparing vegetables and salads long before the meal. Gran, a nutrition nutter, always said that the best green stuff should be culled, cooked and served and not left hanging around. But you have to make compromises in this life and we couldn't leave Ned telly-gawping all day so I washed the mange-tout peas, then I peeled the spuds, layered them with sweet peppers, grated cheese and onion, and poured a mixture of milk and cream over them.

Suddenly, in the middle of all this, Carla said, 'Matty, what am I going to do?'

I swung round surprised and alarmed by the despair in her voice. She was leaning on the kitchen table dropping huge tears on to the stuffed chicken breasts.

I pulled up a chair and eased her into it, then I made us another coffee and sitting down I took her hand and held it tightly.

'I've done everything I can think of,' she sobbed. 'Nothing makes any difference. If only I knew what was wrong. He's hardly ever at home these days and when he is he's so nasty. Perhaps there's another woman.'

I squeezed her hand tighter than ever. 'I shouldn't think so,' I said, amazed at my calm, lying voice. 'He's probably having a rough time at work. Maybe he's worried about his job.'

Hope flickered in her brown eyes. 'You really think that's it and he's not saying anything because he doesn't want to worry me?'

How naive can one person be about another? She knew Giles better than anyone, yet she was still able to kid herself that somewhere under that fake tan lurked a warm, caring husband. Pathetic really but, as I kept reminding myself, it was none of my business.

'Yeah, it'll be something like that.'

'You see,' she said sadly, 'things have been going wrong for some time. I think Giles feels hemmed in by Ned and me.' She tried to laugh. 'He'd probably like to pack his bags and run away to sea! And I do understand it. The world was Giles's playground before we were married.'

It still is, I thought.

'Anyway,' she sniffed miserably, 'you're not a fool. You must have noticed. It's even begun to affect Ned. He's so difficult at the moment.'

To be honest I was completely out of my depth. Knowing the cause of her unhappiness, and being unable to put her in the picture made me feel utterly frustrated and helpless.

'Have you talked it over with your mum?' I asked. 'That's what I do when I get a problem.'

Carla shook her head. 'You haven't met my Mum! She expects us all to live up to the picture she's formed of us. To be unhappy, or to fail in some way is to let the side down. Of course Ned hasn't had time to fail yet so he's the flavour of the century.'

Just talking about it seemed to have restored her energy and she blew her nose, swallowed another moutnful of whiskey and began to look more like her old self. I never knew anyone with such speedy recuperative powers!

'Now who's going to do the tropical fruit salad and who the syllabub?' She asked brightly.

'I'll do the syllabub,' I cried and I jumped up knocking over my chair which fell on top of the cat who leapt up on to the counter, skidded into the tray of milles-feuilles and sent it hurtling to the floor.

Just my lu . . .

'Oh Matty!' Carla doubled up laughing. 'What would I do without you? Don't ever leave me, will you?'

But I was too busy rescuing the milles-feuilles from the jaws of the cat to reply. Anyway, I never make promises I can't keep.

Chapter 11

At last everything was ready. We hadn't had time for much in the way of housework but Carla did brilliant things with a load of greenery and a few chrysanths from the flower shop around the corner. I set the dining room table with the Royal Worcester china, and the Robson's best silver and crystal. I put light blue napkins on to the side plates and dark blue candles into my favourite candlesticks. It looked really smashing.

When it came to my clothes I knew it was no good trying to outshine Diane so I settled for looking cheerful and Christmassy. Raking through my drawers I found a pair of old yellow-satin trousers Mum had used in her act, and teamed them with a baggy scarlet sweater. I swept my hair to one side and stuck an artificial rose in it. My new red shoes pinched a bit but they looked fantastic and it was a good opportunity to wear them in.

After Carla had tucked Ned up for the night she came into my room and had a good look at me. 'Turn around. Yes that's great. The bright lipstick is perfect and I don't know what you've done to your eyes but they look big and shiny.'

Carla doesn't often compliment you so I was quite pleased – not that I had much hope of hooking Harry with Diane around.

Harry and Lion arrived at the same time. Harry, looking very spruce and conventional in a dark suit and tie, presented me with a box of chocs.

'Diane had to meet some film guy for drinks at the Ritz,' he said. 'She'll be along later.'

With any luck, I thought, she won't get here at all!

Lion, in great form, produced a teddy-bear from behind his back, and kissed my cheek. 'Happy birthday kid!', and then whispered, 'I'm really sorry I haven't seen you for a while.'

I smiled. I suppose I'd missed his company recently, but I wasn't pining for him, that's for sure. 'It's Carla's birthday, not mine.'

Lion grabbed back his teddy. 'Then this is for Carla,' he roared and charged off down the corridor in search of her.

June and Sven arrived together. One look at June's remote expression as she limped in told me the kind of mood she was in. I could only hope that the presence of other people would cheer her up a bit. Sven's broad shoulders seemed to fill the entire hall. He wore pale, almost white trousers with a dark jacket and managed to look spectacular and unassuming at the same time. He kissed me warmly.

'I don't know what all this is in aid of but it's a great idea,' he said, putting a bottle of wine on to the hall table.

Fortunately everyone more or less knew everyone else so I was spared doing the introductions and we all trooped into the living room where Carla handed out champagne cocktails. Lion and Sven asked for scotch on the rocks instead. Lion didn't surprise me but Sven usually stuck to wine; in fact I'd never seen him drink spirits, and although he seemed okay I could have sworn that behind his jocular mood he was uneasy, jumpy even. Perhaps June had been giving him an extra hard time? I couldn't help wondering how much longer he'd take it and come back for more.

When everyone had a drink I rapped on a table for silence.

'Today is Carla's birthday,' I said, 'and that's the reason you're all here so I'd like us all to say . . . ' I raised my glass, 'happy birthday Carla.'

It was the first speech I'd ever made but it went down okay and we all drank a toast and sent up a rousing chorus of 'Happy birthday to you.'

Carla, dramatic and beautiful in a navy and red caftan, was very touched and said how super it was of everyone to come and help her celebrate, and how she knew it was going to be a super party and how no one was to worry if she wasn't around much because she was in charge of the kitchen where she'd be having a super time . . . and quite a lot more in the same vein.

A faint twinge of anxiety began plucking at my

stomach. She was talking animatedly but her eyes looked slightly unfocused and she seemed unaware that she'd tilted her glass and was gently dripping champagne on to the carpet. Could she be a bit squiffy? Then I remembered the nips she'd had during the day – whiskey in the morning; sherry at lunch; and a brandy or two at six ('Just to relax me before the party'). Of course I knew that she'd been deeply hurt by Giles forgetting her birthday, and I suppose I should have kept an eye on her, but it never occurred to me that she'd get tanked up – after all, she never had before and it wasn't the first time he'd neglected her. I couldn't help worrying about our carefully prepared dinner but as I'd promised to let her get on with it I just had to try and relax.

Anyway soon we were all dunking pieces of raw veg into a variety of delicious dips and laughing at Lion's account of a rich client who'd insisted on taking six Afghan hounds for a test drive in one of his Mercs, then refused to buy it because, 'I can tell they don't like the colour.'

Even June thought this was quite funny and laughed along with everyone else. I watched her diving into the dip with a raw carrot. She had a truly amazing appetite. What's more, she never put on an ounce. This evening she was wearing a tight-fitting cream floor-length dress – to hide her surgical shoe I suppose – and huge brass earrings the size of hoola-hoops. She looked as if a puff of wind would blow her away but I was beginning to know better. June was as tough as a well-seasoned pair of hiking boots.

I'd managed to plonk myself down next to Harry and while the others were engaged in witty conversation I said, 'How are things going then?' in what I hoped was a low sexy voice.

'I thought you'd be mad at me,' he confessed.

I pretended to be puzzled. 'Why should I?'

'Because I deserted you the other night.'

'Oh that.' I shrugged. 'I guess you thought Diane's need was greater than mine. You were probably right.'

He gave a rueful shake of the head. 'You know Diane.'

Yeah, I knew her all right!

'I bet your place is getting into a mess again,' I said. 'Would you like me to straighten it out tomorrow evening? I could come up after supper.'

He ran his hand indecisively through his hair. 'I'm not sure what I'm doing tomorrow. Can I let you know?'

Oh sure, I thought, when you know exactly what m'lady Diane is doing! For a couple of minutes I felt quite down. It was like beating your head against a soft but immovable object. Thud, thud thud. It didn't exactly hurt but you couldn't get through. Anyway at that moment the door bell pealed and I got up to answer it.

Of course it was Diane and of course she was looking fabulous in purple velvet pants and a loose black top which kept slipping off one creamy shoulder. She was clanking with chunky jewellery and her make-up consisted of sweeping mauve eye-shadow and bright triangles of blusher under her cheek bones. It sounds funny doesn't it? Well I wish it had been. It was fabulous.

'Hi,' she said stepping into the hall. 'This is Charlie. He's come to dinner.'

Chapter 12

No wonder I hadn't noticed him standing behind her. He was about five foot tall, wore a dark suit and was Japanese.

'Hi,' I said, my mind flashing to the seven portions of chicken we had so carefully prepared. Oh well, someone would have to go without seconds.

I expected him to bow but he stuck out his hand in the normal way.

'Nice place you have here,' he said looking round Carla's tatty hall at the stacked grocery boxes, kid's scooters etc.

'It isn't my pl . . . ' I began.

'I told you,' Diane interrupted rudely. 'She's the nanny.'

'Very nice,' he repeated.

They followed me into the living room.

'Here's Diane and she's brought er . . . Charlie,' I said looking desperately at Carla. I needn't have worried. Leaping lightly – if a fraction unsteadily – to her feet Carla shoved the plate of crudités under his nose saying, 'Have a piece of celery. Sorry there isn't any raw fish. Would you like a champagne cocktail?'

'I'd prefer a whiskey,' he said candidly. 'And I can't stand raw fish.'

Lion went off to get him a drink and we all sat down again.

'Charlie's got his own film company,' Diane said draping herself elegantly over one end of the sofa.

Ah so? Clever little Diane!

'Do you know Meryl Streep?' Lion asked coming back with the whiskey.

'I know everyone,' Charlie said modestly.

Diane nodded. 'You wouldn't believe the people he's promised to introduce me to.'

We all looked suitably impressed.

Harry munched a piece of celery noisily. 'And have you got a part for Diane in your next film?'

Charlie eyed him cooly over the rim of his glass. 'It's a possibility.'

Diane rearranged her limbs to greater effect. 'He says I remind him of Carol Lombard.'

'Who's Carol Lombard?' I asked.

She frowned, as if a fly had just settled on her nose, and I realized that she didn't know either.

'She was a movie star,' Lion said. 'Married to Clark Gable – Gone With The Wind and all that – she died in a plane crash.'

'Husband broken-hearted,' Charlie offered, shaking his head sadly.

But Diane was anxious to get the conversation back on a personal level. 'Anyway,' she purred. 'I think it's absolutely sweet of him to think of me.'

'What kind of a part do you want Diane for?' Harry asked.

But Charlie was not going to be trapped into disclosing his plans for his protégé. 'That's still under discussion.'

Diane giggled. 'He wants me to play a Japanese business man's piece of crumpet.'

Lion grinned. 'Perfect casting.'

'Oh really!' She pouted, but a blind man could tell she was pleased.

Harry leaned forward, forcing himself into Charlie's line of vision. 'She won't have to . . . have to . . . *do* anything will she?'

Charlie laughed. Well, I think it was a laugh but it sounded more like a frog croaking. 'Of course she will do something. I'm not going to pay her for sitting still.'

Or lying still, I thought nastily!

'Diane will make a very beautiful film star,' Sven said gallantly and winked at me.

Harry, looking white and angry around the mouth, got up to re-charge the empty glasses. I glanced anxiously at my watch. What with waiting for Diane, then settling Charlie in, the meal was well overdue, yet Carla was still downing champagne cocktails as if we had all the time in the world. When she finally left the room I followed her into the kitchen.

'What are we going to do about the food?' I asked urgently. 'We've only made enough for seven.'

She shrugged carelessly. 'Doesn't matter. Charlie can have mine.'

'Carla no.'

'Matty yes.' She grinned wickedly. 'Like me to add a little arsenic to Diane's portion?'

I groaned. 'She's a real wart. Fancy bringing along another guest at this stage. She didn't even apologise. Harry's looking murderous, and you can't blame the guy.'

'Harry's a real wally,' Carla said removing the foil cover from the milles-feuilles.

'He isn't,' I said sharply. 'He's in love that's all. It does things to a person.'

'Okay, okay. No need to rush to his defence. I know you're soft on him but you're too young to start playing mummy to boys like that. I mean Ned's enough to cope with isn't he?' While speaking she re-filled her champagne glass. I could hardly believe my eyes. If she carried on like this, she'd be flat out before we reached the second course!

'Enough? Sometimes he's too much,' I said curtly. 'Sometimes this whole family is too much!' And plonking the milles-feuilles on to the trolley I trundled it along to the dining room, devoutly wishing I could send everyone home before the evening sprang any more unwelcome surprises.

I don't know if you have ever experienced a feeling that something you are involved with is doomed; that whatever you do won't make any difference? Well that's just how I felt when they all filed into the dining room. To start with I saw June shake off Sven's helping hand and limp aggressively along the corridor under her own steam. Charlie followed, with Diane clinging possessively to his arm. Harry came next, hands thrust into his pockets, eyes angrily on the pair in front of him. Then Lion and Sven, chatting away about some boring motor-show in Paris.

Are all dinner parties like this, I wondered, so staid and middle-aged? I'd imagined it would all be such fun. How wrong can you get?

The first course went fairly well. Charlie kept up a steady monologue on the state of the Japanese film industry and we all listened respectfully until Harry rudely interrupted him mid-flow:

'The trouble with you people is that you are fighting another war.'

It was as if someone had deliberately pulled a drawstring and tightened the atmosphere. All eyes switched to Harry's pale, angry face and back to Charlie's bland, smiling mask.

Charlie reacted mildly enough. 'What do you mean Harry? We are only just recovering from the last one.'

'You know what I mean. An economic war; what's

more you are winning, hands down. In the end we'll all be dancing to the music of your bloody computers.'

'Harry you're raving,' Diane said.

Charlie smiled kindly. 'You do not like us Japanese?'

Harry had the grace to look slightly embarrassed. 'Of course I like Japanese people . . . '

'I think you're very rude,' Diane interrupted crossly. 'Charlie's our guest you know.'

Harry glared at her. 'Your guest I believe, and I'm sure he can stand up for himself.'

'Matty, the milles-feuilles were delicious,' Sven said briefly laying a hand over mine. 'Worthy of a Michelin rosette.' I looked into his smiling eyes.

'Thanks. They were a speciality of my Gran's.' Sven always had the knack of making me feel special, which is more than could be said for Harry.

Fortunately everyone had finished eating, so conversation stopped while he and I collected the plates and carted them out to the kitchen, where we found Carla ineffectually attempting to lay out the chicken on a serving dish. It was obvious by now that she was getting rather drunk.

'Let me do it,' I said pushing her out of the way before she could ruin everything. Sven plonked her (giggling like a fool) on to a chair and we piled the chicken breasts and stuff on to the dish and then on to the trolley. Half way along the passage I ground to a halt and looked round at Sven.

'What's the matter with her?' I asked in a stage whisper. 'In fact what's the matter with everyone?' But he gave me an impatient little push in the back. 'Nothing's the matter. The food's delicious. You are looking very pretty and I'm enjoying myself.'

'I'm glad someone is,' I said shakily.

In the dining room Lion and Charlie were discussing the government's handling of Land Rover, June was gazing into space and Diane and Harry were having a row about a party she didn't want to go to the following evening. Charlie was looking orientally inscrutable.

'You promised,' Harry said.

Diane scowled (it made her look really ugly). 'Don't be such a bore Harry.'

I listened, my heart in my mouth. How could they go on like this at my party? I thought people went to parties to get away from their personal problems and have a good time. This lot seemed intent on sorting themselves out in public. Anyway I tried to ignore the atmosphere and concentrated on seeing that everyone had enough to eat. Though I say it myself, the food was delicious, the table looked pretty and the candles cast such a gentle glow over the guests that, just for a moment while they were all tucking into their chicken, I thought the situation might recover. Then, out of the blue, June said,

'I'm leaving for the States on Friday week to have an operation on my foot.'

A murmur of surprise and approval ran around the table. I glanced at Sven who put down his knife and fork and stared incredulously at her. 'But I thought you'd given up the idea.'

June sipped her wine. 'Well I've changed my mind.' She shot him a triumphant look. 'No reason why I shouldn't is there?'

'None at all, but Matty's party isn't the place to discuss it.'

June banged her glass furiously on to the table slopping wine over the edge. 'You never think anywhere is the place to discuss anything important!'

He shook his head warningly. 'June please . . . '

'Oh sod off!' she said angrily.

Charlie turned to Diane. 'You would like to go to the States Diane? Maybe we can do a film there!

'Fantastic,' she breathed, inclining her boobs towards him.

Harry half rose from his chair and I saw Sven quickly stretch out a hand to stop him. Suddenly we heard a noise in the corridor and we all looked round. Carla, stately and magnificent in her red and blue robe, the final strains of Some Enchanted Evening on her lips, bore down on us through the open door, a tray of tall syllabub-glasses professionally balanced on the fingers of one hand.

'Everyone ready for pudding?' she carolled, then she tripped on the rug and the glasses hurtled into the room sending a cascade of creamy syllabub all over Diane and Charlie who were sitting nearest to the door. There was a moment of stunned silence then Lion said, 'This is turning into quite a party,' and he burst out laughing.

Chapter 13

He was wrong. The episode promptly and efficiently put paid to the rest of the evening. Diane and Charlie, smothered with syllabub, were whisked away to be cleaned up by Harry and June – Diane squawking like an offended chicken – while Sven and I attended to Carla who was sitting on the floor clutching her ankle, moaning quietly. There was no question of going on with the meal. Glass was everywhere, fine crystal splinters glinted in the butter and in the food on the plates (we hadn't quite finished when Carla made her dramatic entrance) and on the rug that had caused the whole thing. Glancing frantically around I had visions of Giles's wrath when he discovered what had happened. The champagne glasses we had used for the syllabub were a wedding present from the president of his company. Would he blame me or Carla for the accident?

Not that I had much time to think about it as I had to concentrate on poor Carla who held my hand tightly and sobbed, 'Oh Matty I've made such a mess of the whole thing and I did so want it to be a happy occasion.'

She was so miserable that my anger and disappointment fell away like a discarded cloak and I put my arms around her and tried to comfort her.

'Don't be daft, we'll look back on this and have a good laugh.' I tried to pull her to her feet. 'Come on. Let's get you to bed.'

Glancing up I caught Sven staring at me with an odd mixture of amusement and approval and – strangely – tenderness. He looked away as our eyes met and called Lion who was attempting to clear up the broken glass. Between the three of us we helped Carla along to her room. Her ankle was already quite swollen so we got her onto her bed and I applied a cold compress and made her as comfortable as possible, then left her to sleep it off.

When I finally emerged from the bedroom the flat

was deserted except for Sven who was in the kitchen, in his shirt sleeves, stacking the dish-washer.

'How's Carla?' he asked.

I shrugged wearily. 'She'll be okay in the morning. Where is everyone?'

'They've all gone.'

'Gone? Without finishing dinner or saying goodbye?'

'Yes.' He lifted the foil cover off the untouched fruit salad. 'This looks good. Want some?'

I shook my head.

He replaced the foil. 'Diane was determined to leave so Lion offered to drive her and Charlie back to the Ritz, and June was tired so Harry did escort duty.'

'Harry?' I said sharply.

He threw me a wry smile. 'Sorry Matty. She wouldn't let me. I did try.'

'Yeah, sure.' For the first time I felt like crying. Harry hadn't even stayed behind to help me clean the place up. You'd have thought that after watching Diane fawn over Charlie all evening he'd have realized that he hadn't a hope. But no, the idiot couldn't wait to get away and plan the next romantic supper for two – or whatever – so he'd seized the opportunity of June's and Sven's row to see June home.

For some odd reason I began to feel extraordinarily cross with Sven. He should have insisted on taking June home himself. She was his responsibility and he should have over-ridden her rotten temper.

'Perhaps you'd like to go now too,' I said crisply.

He looked surprised. 'Me? No I'll stay and help.

I shook my head. 'Thanks but I'd rather be alone.'

Sven's blue eyes widened. 'You don't really mean that Matty?'

I could feel my face going all hard, like it does when you apply one of those cosmetic masks. 'I wouldn't say it if I didn't.'

He flushed and lifted his jacket off the back of a chair. 'Okay, okay. This seems to be my night for getting the big brush off.'

I didn't reply. Instead I marched along the corridor and opened the front door wide. Sven paused in the doorway, a troubled expression on his kind face, but I just stared coldly at him and he left silently.

Why do I do these things? It's happened more than once in my life. Someone extends a much-needed helping hand and I bite off their fingers. It's so stupid because as soon as I've done it I regret it. After Sven had gone I sat on the hall chair and had a little cry. Well, a large cry really. It wasn't only the disastrous evening, it was the disturbing undercurrents that ran through everyone's lives. Perhaps the best thing would be to give in my notice and go home. Of course Mum and Dad wouldn't be too pleased, but if I stuck around here much longer I might start to be affected by the unhappy atmosphere and get even more depressed than I already was. London had definitely changed me. I no longer felt so, I don't know, carefree I suppose. Instead of taking things at face value I'd begun to wonder what lay beneath the surface and I'd started questioning people's motives, all too often arriving at disturbing conclusions. City people were definitely not what they seemed and I wondered whether it was due to pressures unknown to country people, or because I'd taken a mental leap forward and begun to see the whole of life in a more realistic light?

But my brain was too tired to think it out properly

and I wanted to get the place straight before morning, so I stuck a Beat Boys tape into my recorder, clamped on my headphones and headed for the kitchen. Oh Sven, I thought, looking at the chaos, why did I let you go?

I never did find out what Giles said about the champagne glasses. I imagine Carla told him she had given a party and had accidently broken them. I bet she didn't tell him that it was my party! Anyway things between them certainly didn't improve and the only reason I didn't hand in my notice was Carla's misery. Her ankle got better pretty quickly but she seemed to have lost all her spirit and left for work in the morning looking fagged out and returned looking worse. I just couldn't run out on her. When she asked me if I'd like to go home for Christmas I said yes but it was still three weeks away and I shelved the decision of whether or not to stay there permanently until nearer the time. After all, I reasoned, anything could happen between now and then: Giles could chuck his lady friend and return to Carla's loving arms; Harry could even get the final message about Diane and set his sights on yours truly. Well, anyone can dream can't they?

Soon after the party Lion telephoned and said it was the funniest evening of his life. (That made me feel great I can tell you!) June sent a pot of African violets and a note – which I ignored – asking me to come down and see her. Diane sent the cleaner's bill for her black silk top – which Carla paid – and Harry put his head in the door and said he was sorry things had turned out so badly and if I felt like cleaning up his flat sometime he'd be very pleased as his daily had departed in a huff. I didn't hear from Sven at all.

After that I didn't see any of them for a while. Anyway, I had to concentrate on buying Christmas presents and helping Ned make cards and gifts for his parents and grandparents. As a matter of fact Ned seemed to improve as Christmas approached. I suppose the lights and the glitzy shop windows and trips to Harrods' and Selfridge's toy departments all took his mind off the atmosphere at home.

I expect things would have gone on as usual if it hadn't been for the weekend Carla and Giles decided to take Ned to visit Giles's brother in York. Ned had just recovered from a tummy-bug, and on the Sunday I got it.

Now I am not a very brave person and the thing I am un-bravest about is illness. I can't bear being ill alone. So when I woke up that morning and recognized the symptoms I panicked. You see I am one of those people who gets things like that really badly. I've been known to pass out – not once but several times. But what was I to do? I mean you don't call the doctor or go to the hospital *before* you are ill – they'd think you were mad. And Mrs Belasco would hardly welcome me being sick in her immaculate guest room – even if June was prepared to look after me. If I'd had a more stoic nature I suppose I'd have suffered alone but I haven't, so I stuck it out until I began to feel really desperate then I crawled upstairs to Harry.

He opened the door still wearing his pyjamas and looked me over distastefully. 'Oh Lord, you've got it now!'

'Yeah.' I leaned weakly against the door-post. 'Can I stay?'

He didn't look too happy. 'I suppose so.'

'After all, you are going to be a doctor.'

'Yes, well you'd better come . . . ' but I was already through the door and heading for the bathroom for the fourth session of a very long day.

After his initial hesitation he was amazing. He put me into his parents' bed – a vast affair with a gilded headboard – and nipped downstairs to collect my nightdress and washing things. I was vaguely aware of him moving around the room and occasionally dabbing my forehead with something damp and eau-de-Cologny, but most of the time I was only conscious of my misery and the cold white bowl of the loo and the hands of the clock by the bed as they crept slowly around the face of the dial. Eight hours. I always retch my heart out for eight hours. For the next four I lie there tossing and turning, aching in every muscle, then comes a short, blissful period when I know I am going to live and I can take sips of water and enjoy being waited on. Then I sleep and wake up better. That's it, and it was no different this time. So when ten o'clock at night rolled around there I was, in the big bed, all washed and brushed and smelling like an eau-de-Cologne factory, gazing gratefully up at an exhausted Harry. I remember feeling sort of high – empty and light-headed.

'When you get it I'll do the same for you,' I promised.

He grinned. 'I'll keep you to that.'

I sighed contentedly. 'It's great to be feeling better.'

'I bet.' He sat on the bed and took my limp hand in his. 'I was quite worried about you.'

'Really?' I smiled teasingly. 'I didn't know you cared.'

'Of course I do,' he said seriously. 'You're such a fish out of water in London – so naive and trusting. I'm always afraid something awful will happen to you.'

'Like what?'

'I don't know. Rape or something. You're too friendly with strangers. It's probably okay in the country, but not here.'

I could hardly believe my ears. Perhaps the night of the party had finally brought him to his senses regarding Diane. Perhaps there was a good chance for me now? They always say there's nothing like illness to show you where your heart really lies.

'I've never even been propositioned let alone raped,' I laughed, and pushing myself up in the bed I locked my hands behind my head. I was wearing this very pretty flowered nightie made of gauzy material and I saw his eyes travel to my boobs.

'That's quite surprising,' he said in a croaky sort of voice.

'Is it?' I whispered gazing deeply into his eyes, then he sort of leaned down and I sort of sat up and we met in the middle. His lips were dry and warm and his shoulders, under my exploring fingers, felt thin and boyish. We kissed for a long time and gradually I sank back on to the pillows taking him with me then he got his legs on to the bed and we lay there in each other's arms, Harry on top and me under the duvet.

'You smell lovely,' he said.

'Your mother's eau-de-Cologne.'

'She won't mind.'

'Not even when she knows I was in her bed?'

'Well she won't know will she?'

I traced the side of his jaw with my finger. The bone felt padded and springy and the skin smooth, quite different to Lion's hard, bristly face. 'I've been longing for you to kiss me,' I murmured.

He smiled. 'Have you? Shall I do it again?'

'Please!' I tightened my arms around his neck and pressed myself to him through the duvet. This time we kissed for even longer; he seemed terribly hungry for kissing, kind of starved in fact, and I had to break away in order to breathe.

'Oh you're so lovely,' he said nuzzling my neck.

'You wouldn't have said that a few hours ago when I was being sick.'

'Things like that don't bother a doctor.'

'But you're not a doctor ye . . . '

'Shut up,' he said and stopped my mouth with another long kiss. I heard his shoes drop on to the floor and felt him tugging at the duvet and somehow, without me doing anything to help, he was in the bed with me, his woolly socks scratching my bare feet. I clung to him, my heart beating fit to burst, my whole body humming like Ned's spinning-top.

'I love you,' I whispered. 'Oh Harry, I do love you.'

'Oh Diane . . . ' he groaned and began pulling at the neck of my nightdress.

I froze. He didn't seem to notice but went on fumbling with my buttons, his eyes tightly shut.

'I'm not Diane,' I said fiercely. 'I'm Matty!'

He opened his eyes. 'What?'

'You called me Diane.'

He drew back a little. 'Did I?'

'Yeah.'

'Well . . . ' he smiled vaguely. 'Never mind.' And he pulled me close again.

I pushed him away. 'But I do mind. I thought this meant you'd finished with her.'

'What meant?'

'All this kissing and stuff.'

'Finished with Diane?'

'Yeah. Haven't you? It's important. I mean we're, well . . . here, in your parent's bed, aren't we?'

He suddenly let out a long sigh and flopped back on to the pillows. 'Oh God. Yes we are.'

'So you haven't finished with her?'

There was a brief, heart-stopping pause then he shook his head.

I slipped out of bed and stood looking down at him. 'Then why all the love-making? Were you pretending that I was her or something?'

'No of course not. You're very attractive – you must know that by now – but Diane never . . . I mean she never . . . ' His voice tailed away but I knew what he meant all right. Diane never let him near her body-beautiful so I was the next best thing. It's well known that all cats look grey at night I thought bitterly.

I began to shiver and my legs started to tremble weakly. In a flash Harry was out of the bed and I was back in it. He bashed up the pillows and tucked the duvet around me. I turned on my side and closed my eyes. Neither of us said a word. I heard him go out of the room then return and put something down on my bed-side table – by the sound of it my water-jug. Then I felt him drop a kiss on my left temple.

'I'm sorry Matty. You deserve better.'

The light went out. The door closed. It was over.

Chapter 14

I slept like a log and woke early with something on my mind. Then I remembered. Harry. Lying in his mother's bed with the duvet pulled up under my chin I imagined his body against mine: his bony shoulder blades and ribs; his warm breath on my face; the buckle of his belt pressing into my tummy. I shivered. If he hadn't murmured 'Diane' like that I would probably have let him unbutton my nightie. In fact this morning I half regretted not having done so. On the other hand if we'd gone too far and afterwards I'd found out that he was still hot for Diane I'd have been even more hurt than I already was.

I wondered how he was feeling this morning. Ashamed and guilty? Probably; he was too nice to want to hurt me deliberately. One thing was certain – he wouldn't want to see me until he'd had time to get himself together so I'd better dress quickly and make myself scarce before he appeared.

I seemed to have lost weight over the past 24 hours because my cords almost fell off my hips but, apart from a slight tenderness in the tummy area and a ravenous hunger, I felt none the worse for the gastric attack. While I was doing up my shirt I heard the radio start up in Harry's room and realized that he would soon begin moving around and my chance of escape would be lost. After hastily twitching the duvet into place I dived for the door, crept along the passage and let myself out of the flat.

Carla and Ned arrived back at tea-time. Ned seemed to have enjoyed himself and insisted on dressing up in the cowboy outfit his uncle had given him, but Carla looked exhausted. She had big grey shadows under her eyes and although she tried to be cheerful I could tell it was all put on. She immediately disappeared into her bedroom to have a rest leaving me to cook supper and amuse Ned. She seemed to rest an awful lot these days; in fact from time to time I thought she looked quite ill but she never complained, so we didn't talk about it. She hadn't mentioned her problems with Giles since my awful party and although my heart went out to her I just didn't know how to help.

Ned was in bed and the dinner was almost ready when Giles came in.

'Fish again?' he said sourly, poking his head into the kitchen.

But I was determined to be pleasant. 'Your favourite. Truite aux amandes.'

He grinned. 'Show off!'

I grinned insincerely back. 'Yeah, that's me.'

We sat down ten mintues later. Giles had changed into a blue sweater which made his eyes look like a couple of blue glass paperweights and his hair looked so blond that I wondered if he'd had it tinted. I mean you can't tell these days. Carla, although quiet, seemed in slightly better spirits and they nattered away, peaceably enough, about the weekend in York and about their plans for Christmas.

'I'll drive Ned down to Mum's on Christmas Eve morning,' Carla said.

For once Giles agreed. 'You do that. I've got the office party at midday so I'll come down later in the Audi.'

'Then you'll bring the luggage and I'll take all Ned's clobber?'

'Right.' Giles fixed me with a glassy eye. 'When are you going home Matty?'

'The day before you.'

He looked at Carla. 'Why? I mean why isn't she staying to help pack up?'

'She is,' Carla said. 'Everything will be ready by Christmas Eve. Matty has quite a long train journey so I've given her an extra day off.'

'I don't see that that's necessary.'

Carla pushed her fish irritably to one side. 'Well that's what we've arranged.'

He clamped his lips together in a thin line. 'I pay Matty you know. You don't.'

I could see Carla beginning to steam so I said, 'I'll stay until you go if you like.' I mean, anything to keep the peace.

'No!' Carla said sharply. 'We'll leave it as it is.'

Giles opened his mouth to retort but the door bell rang.

'I'll go,' I said half rising, but he threw down his table napkin and stomped to the door.

He was back in seconds carrying a plastic bag. 'This was on the mat.'

'It's probably a bomb,' I joked.

O my prophetic soul! Someone famous said that; I can't remember who it was but it's very apt in this case. Opening up the bag Giles peered inside then exclaimed, 'What the hell . . . ?' and pulled out my night-dress followed by my face-cloth and toothbrush. We all gazed at them.

'Er . . . those are mine,' I said blushing to the roots of my hair.

Carla twigged at once and did her level best to get me off the hook.

'Well put them down Giles and get on with your dinner, before it freezes over.' Picking up her knife and fork she tackled the remains of her fish. 'Now what were we talking about before all that? Ah yes. Christmas.'

'Just a minute.' Giles stood at the end of the table frowning, the wretched bag suspended from his forefinger. 'How did these things get here Matty? Who brought them?'

'Oh Giles!' Carla groaned. 'What does it matter?'

'It matters very much.' He stared stonily at me. 'Well?'

I took a deep breath. There was no point in lying. After all it was my life; it wasn't up to him to say what I could and couldn't do. 'Harry must have brought them.'

'Harry who?'

'Harry Lord,' Carla said in a resigned voice. 'The son of the diplomatic types in number 15.'

'But aren't they in Hong Kong or somewhere?'

'I think so.' She waved casually at his plate. 'Giles do finish your trout.'

'Not until I get to the bottom of this. What were your night-things doing in this boy's flat?'

'I got Ned's bug,' I muttered, 'so Harry put me into his parent's bed and looked after me.'

'Oh my God!' He gave a really nasty laugh. 'His parent's bed! A truly exquisite touch. Did you know about this Carla?'

'No, but if Matty says . . . '

'Really Carla – how gullible can you get? No wonder your company has been losing money lately. If they're all as naive as you . . . '

Alarmed by the venom he was directing as much at

Carla as at me I sat clutching my chair-seat, watching his face get redder and redder. Why wouldn't he listen? And why take it out on Carla? It was so unfair because it had nothing to do with her. Poor Carla. Her head was bent over her plate and I could tell she was about to burst into tears. She was already so miserable that I really couldn't bear it and before I knew what I was doing I banged my fist on the table making the knives and forks jump about like fleas.

'It's true!' I shouted. 'I *was* ill. I needed help and went up to Harry. That's all there was to it.' (Well nearly all.)

They both looked at me as if they'd forgotten I was there, then Giles shook his head. 'God Matty – you must think I was born yesterday! Why not just admit you took advantage of our absence to leap into bed with young Lord and we can take it from there?'

'Giles . . . ' Carla began.

He turned on her savagely. 'Shut up! I bet this has been going for weeks and you've condoned the whole thing. What sort of a mother are you? You wanted children – I didn't then and don't now – but you don't want to take care of them yourself. That would be too much like hard work. So you nip off and get yourself a cushy ego-stroking job and import this little tramp to look after your son. I warned you about her months ago but you insisted on keeping her. Now perhaps you'll admit I was right.'

Carla leapt to her feet. 'I'll admit nothing of the kind. If Matty says she was ill then I believe her. As for my job – you're exhibiting a particularly nasty professional jealousy . . .

'Ha!' (from Giles)

'What do you want me to do? Stay at home and stare

at the four walls while you jet around the world on a huge expense account, popping home occasionally to find fault with the way I've ironed the table napkins? And what do you mean I don't want to look after my own son? What about you? When did you last spend a weekend at home with him? Take him to the park? Read to him? Play with him? He's terrified of you. Did you know that? When he hears your key in the door he runs to his room. Your own son is scared stiff of you Giles. How do you like that? Makes you feel big does it?'

I sat frozen to my chair, appalled by the hate in their voices. How could something that started out with my night-gear turn into a row about what kind of parents they were? It didn't make sense. Nothing about this place made sense any longer. I stood up.

'I think I'll just . . . '

Giles stretched out a long arm and shoved me down again. 'No you don't. This time we'll settle things properly. I won't have my son corrupted by people like you . . . '

Something inside me twanged like a piece of snapped elastic and I heard myself yelling, 'At least I'm not cheating on my wife!'

Giles let out his breath in a long audible hiss. 'What did you say?'

Scrambling out of my seat I moved behind my chair ready to retreat through the door. 'Nothing.'

Giles folded his arms menacingly. 'I should hope not.'

The air vibrated with unspoken threats.

'What did you mean Matty?' Carla's voice spanned acres of polished mahogany.

'She didn't mean anything,' Giles said still staring at

me. 'Go to your room Matty. I'll talk to you later.'

'No.' Carla held up her hand. 'I want to know exactly what Matty meant.'

I stared at her. There were sleepless bags under her eyes; her hair, usually so shiny, hung lank and dull on her neck; her grey face looked slack and lined. I could see exactly what she would be like when she was sixty and lonely and disillusioned. My nails bit into the wood of the chair. It mustn't happen. It really mustn't. There was still time. Now she might still have a chance . . .

'Matty!' Carla seized the edge of the table and leaned towards me. 'I am your friend. I've always tried to help you. Now you must help me. If not me then Ned. This situation is making us both ill. Please . . . '

'Don't be stupid,' Giles blustered. 'You don't know what you're saying. Anyway you can't believe a girl like this . . . '

'Matty . . . '

I gripped the chair-back and looked deep into her eyes. They reminded me of Bambi's eyes in the Disney film – big and brown and vulnerable.

'They were at the Peregrine Hotel in Exeter,' I blurted out. 'Lion and I saw them. She was very attractive but sort of hard looking. They often stay there. He signs in as Geoffrey Roebuck.'

'How do you know?' Carla whispered.

'Jan told me. She's a friend of Lion's and she owns the place . . . ' My voice trailed away.

Silence, except for the striking of the grandfather clock in the hall. Dong . . . dong . . . dong . . . my numb brain began to chant the old nursery rhyme – Hickory dickory dock, the mouse ran up the clock . . .

'You little BITCH . . . !' Giles leapt at me but I was

ready for him, and diving under the table I came up the other side, sprang through the open door and sprinted down the passage into my room, and slammed and locked the door.

Giles hurled himself at the door swearing blue murder but it was one of those old fashioned jobs with a bolt as well as a lock so, hoping for the best, I got into bed, pulled the covers over my head, stuck my fingers in my ears and stayed there.

I remember Dad telling me that his father had told him that, during the air raids, many people had slept soundly with bombs raining around them like hail stones. Of course I didn't believe him. I mean how could you sleep knowing the next moment could be your last? But now I know he was right. While Giles was still battering my door I fell asleep. I must have conked right out because when I awoke the front door bell was ringing and it was dark and my clock said eleven-thirty.

I heard Carla's footsteps running along the corridor, then I heard strange excited voices and the sound of Carla crying, then they must have gone into the living room and closed the door because everything went quiet.

My first thought was Ned. Had he slept through the uproar or was he lying awake too terrified to move? Getting out of bed I gently turned the key in my lock, drew back the bolt and stepped into the passage. No one was around and I was about to go along to Ned's room when a noise in the entrance hall made me peek around the corner. There was Ned, fully dressed in out-door gear, with his favourite toy engine under one arm, half way through the open door.

'Ned,' I said softly, not wanting to frighten him.

He turned and I'll never forget the look of apprehension on his small white face. Then he gave a funny little nod of confidence. 'Oh it's you Matty.'

'Yeah it's me. What are you doing?'

He put his finger to his lips. 'Ssh. They'll hear. I'm running away. Want to come with me?'

Chapter 15

I thought rapidly. 'Okay. Why not?'

He beckoned. 'Come on then.'

'Can't we get together a bit of grub first?'

'I'm not hungry.'

'You will be in the morning. People never run away without food.'

'Chocolate chip cookies?'

'Sure.'

'Okay.' Running back he thrust his hand into mine and we tiptoed along the corridor, ignoring the buzz of voices in the living-room, and shut ourselves into the kitchen.

'How about having a banana milk-shake right now?' I asked hopefully.

I could see he was tempted. 'Okay. But we mustn't be long or they'll find us.

I stuck a straw into Ned's drink and settled him at the table. 'Where are we running to?'

'Grannie's.' He took a long pull through the straw

then wiped his mouth with his hand. 'They don't fight there.'

'Won't you miss Mummy?'

'She'll come and live with us,' he said confidently. 'You can too if you like.'

I sat down opposite him. 'But what about poor Daddy? Who'll look after him?'

He seemed not to have heard. 'Grandad's going to buy me a two-wheeler for my birthday.' Clearly the subject of Daddy was not up for discussion.

As soon as he finished his drink he clambered off his chair and headed for the door, but before he got there it swung open and a woman I'd never seen before came in.

'Grannie!' shouted Ned rushing into her arms. 'Can I come and live with you? Can Matty come too?'

Mrs Markham was a big handsome woman, like Carla. 'Of course you can darling,' she said, all smiles. 'Is that why you're fully dressed at this time of night? Were you coming to see Grannie and Grandad?' She threw me an enquiring look over the top of his head.

I nodded. 'We were just packing some chocolate chip cookies for the journey. You know – in case we got hungry.'

'I see. Well that must have been a lovely game.'

Although she resembled Carla: same build, same dark colouring turned slightly sallow, she lacked Carla's sweetness of expression and looked an altogether tougher version of her daughter.

'Now Matty's going to put you back to bed,' she said firmly, 'and in the morning we'll pack your things and drive down to Strawberry House.'

'Will Mummy come too?'

'Perhaps. We'll see.'

'And Matty?'

She laughed and put her finger against his mouth. 'What an old chatter-box you are. Now off you go with Matty and when you're in bed Mummy will come and tuck you in.'

She put him down and I took his hand. 'Okay soldier, let's go.' We moved towards the door.

'Matty . . . ' I turned. Ned's grandmother eyed me stonily. 'When you've finished in the nursery would you come to the living-room? I know it's late but I'd like a word with you.'

'Right,' I said, but my heart sank at the prospect.

Ned went down with no trouble and was asleep before I tucked the duvet around him. As I was about to leave Carla came in. She looked terrible.

'I found him going out of the front door,' I whispered. 'He was running away.'

We stood looking down at him, then Carla knelt by the bed and began to stroke his hair very lightly while big unheeded tears slid down her cheeks.

It was a private moment so I slipped quietly from the room.

It seemed odd that all the lights in the flat were still blazing so late at night – or so early in the morning – but this was probably the oddest night of my life anyway. Giles's study door was shut and hearing the murmur of men's voices inside I wondered what sons-in-law and fathers-in-law said to each other at times like this. Perhaps they got all the unpleasantness over quickly and went on to the World Cup or something. Perhaps they secretly sympathized with each other's predicament and the role each of them was expected to play – outraged father; guilty husband. By now I knew that nothing is as clear cut as it seems.

Mrs Markham was waiting in the living room. Although she looked yellow with exhaustion she sat rigidly straight on the sofa and fixed me with a gimlet eye.

'Ah Matty.' She waved me to a chair. 'This is a bad business.'

'Yeah.'

'You do realize that my daughter is pregnant?'

I sat bolt upright. 'What? Who? Carla?'

'Yes. She's just at the delicate stage and she's already had two miscarriages since Ned's arrival. This whole storm in a teacup couldn't have come at a worse time.'

Storm in a teacup? Is that what it was? 'But she never said anything about being pregnant to me.'

She raised her eyebrows. 'Why should she? She'd have told you in due course. Anyway, I expect she didn't want to raise false hopes.'

'Does Giles know?'

'He does now.'

'It's true – about him having an affair,' I blurted out, desperately wanting to justify myself. 'I saw them together in Devon. I even checked the hotel register.'

Her shoulders lifted in a superior shrug. 'I've no doubt. But are you really so young, so naive that you imagine all marriages are perfect, all husbands and wives faithful to each other?'

'No but . . . '

'Because if you are you've got a few shocks coming to you. May I ask why you didn't keep this knowledge to yourself? You must have realized no good would come of, so to speak, letting the cat out of the bag.'

I hung my head. 'I kept it to myself for quite a while but Giles accused me of . . . of . . . '

'Of what?'

'Well it's a long story but you see I got ill and had to go for help to the flat upstairs . . . '

'To Archibald and Marina Lord? I know them well, but I thought they were abroad.'

'They are but Harry is living there.'

'Harry? Oh yes. Rather a lonely boy as I recall. Had some idea of becoming a doctor. So you went to him for assistance?'

'Yeah and he put me to bed and looked after me, but when I left this morning I forgot to collect my night things so Harry dumped them outside the front door during supper and Giles found them and . . . '

'Accused you of immoral behaviour?'

'Something like that.'

'Whereupon you lost your temper and out it all came.'

I nodded unhappily. 'It wasn't only that. You see Carla's been miserable for so long and I've been really worried about her.'

'I see.' She closed her eyes and went all silent on me but just as I was wondering whether the interview was over and I could slip away they suddenly snapped open. 'I realize I have absolutely no right to question you like this, but you must understand my position. If this marriage collapses – partly, let it be said, because of your intervention – we, the grandparents, will be left literally holding the baby. And there's no earthly reason for this to happen. Giles is a good provider. Carla wants for nothing . . . '

Nothing except love!

' . . . For everyone's sake I must do everything I can to effect a reconciliation. And that means I have to understand the situation – which is why I asked to see you.'

I leaned forward. 'Giles was wrong. I didn't, you know . . . with Harry.'

She clucked impatiently. 'My dear child! I don't give a hoot whether you did or you didn't. What matters now is the result of your outburst. If Carla has another miscarriage . . . '

'It's unfair to blame me!' I said fiercely. 'You must have known she was unhappy. It's no good papering over the cracks. Things have to be faced.'

She half smiled and shook her head. 'This passion for facing things! I'm not certain it's always the wisest course. Some things do go away.'

'Until the next time.'

She didn't like that. 'Yes well . . . anyway Carla's got to see reason. Most men have the odd affair and it's a wise woman who ignores it. We don't go in for divorce in our family. We stick things out. It generally comes right in the end.'

'Well, whatever Carla and Giles decide, something's got to be done about Ned,' I said, amazed at my own courage. 'He's unhappy and disturbed.'

She frowned as if I'd said something impertinent. 'What on earth do you mean? He seems all right to me, a jolly little chap in fact. I expect the noise woke him up this evening, that's all. Goodness, how you young people exaggerate.'

'I'm not exaggerating. Just after you arrived tonight he tried to run away. I caught him going through the front door.'

A brown-spotted hand flew to her throat. 'Is this true?'

'Of course.'

She sighed and shook her head. 'Well I warned Carla about taking on a nanny with no experience and it seems I was right.'

I gaped with astonishment. 'So that's my fault too?'

'Not your fault exactly but if you'd been a little older, had a little more experience . . . '

I stood up. 'Thanks for the vote of confidence. All you seem to be concerned with is not getting stuck with the whole stinking mess yourself. Carla once told me that she always had to pretend everything was okay because you can't bear things going wrong. Well if you'd supported her when she needed you instead of making her feel utterly alone with her troubles, she might have been able to cope with all this.'

The more I said, the braver I became and I stepped forward, my eyes fairly blazing with anger. 'If you'd like to know, I've really done my best for this family and I'm not going to stay and take stick for things that have nothing to do with me. You'd better look around for another scapegoat, Mrs Markham, and I suggest you try the real culprit – your pig of a son-in-law.' She gasped, and I marched out of the room without waiting for a reply.

As I reached my bedroom the grandfather clock in the hall struck one. Hickory dickory dock . . .

Chapter 16

It took me exactly ten minutes to throw my stuff into a couple of bags, deposit my keys on the hall table and let myself out of the flat. To hell with the lot of them! I felt guilty about not saying goodbye to Carla but with everything in such confusion I would simply be adding to her worries. Naturally I would write later explaining that, with her mother feeling I was responsible for the whole horrible mess, I couldn't possibly stay.

My stuff was quite heavy so I bumped it all the way down stairs hoping nothing inside would break, and it wasn't until I reached the glass entrance doors that I realized I hadn't the faintest idea where to go. Dumping the bags on the ground I stared out at the street. It was raining again. People said you didn't notice the weather so much in London. Wrong. When it rains in the country it seems natural, part of nature's amazing cycle, but in London it simply produces dirty muck instead of clean muck.

I could either brave the rain, muggers and rapists and go in search of an insomniac taxi (oh why didn't I telephone one before I left the flat?) then sit it out at the station, or I could settle down in the entrance hall and wait until it got light. On the whole the latter course seemed preferable so I curled up on the floor under a dusty rubber plant and tried to sleep. I must have succeeded because the next thing I knew someone was shaking my shoulder and opening my eyes I found myself staring into Sven's anxious face.

'Matty? What are you doing here? What's happened?'

I sat up. 'There's been an awful row. I've left the Robsons.'

'You mean they sacked you? In the middle of the night?'

'No. I didn't want to stay any longer.'

'But you can't stay here. It's cold.'

I shivered. 'Yeah but it's too early to catch a train

and I've nowhere to go.'

He pulled me to my feet. 'Come on. We'll find you somewhere.'

'But where?'

He picked up the bags. 'Never mind. Just come with me.'

He hailed a lonely taxi in the Fulham Road and it dropped us outside a small hotel in one of those railed garden-squares in Kensington.

'Is this where you live?' I asked looking nervously at the words 'Helston Lodge' above the portico.

'It is.' He dumped my bags on the top step and got out his key.

'Won't they object to me?'

'Don't fuss,' he said severely. 'It's better than the station isn't it?'

'Yeah but . . . '

'Ssh. We don't want to wake up the whole place.' He shepherded me into the house and up several flights of stairs.

'Bathroom's on the half-landing,' he said, unlocking the door of number 12, and in we went.

It was quite a large room, very mannish and old fashioned. It had stripy wall paper, dark red curtains, a bed with a mahogany headboard, a leather armchair facing the gas fire, and one of those large cupboards which have shelves as well as hanging space. That's all except for a desk-computer and books and papers scattered everywhere. Sven immediately turned on the gas fire.

'The central heating goes off at night.'

I wandered over to the window. 'At least you're up high.'

'On a clear day you can see Harrods.'

'You're kidding!' I gave a rueful laugh. 'Not that a week in Harrods with unlimited cash would do much for me right now.'

'Poor Matty.' He drew the armchair closer to the fire. 'Come and relax and tell me what happened.'

And because I trusted him completely I did, starting with the night I'd spent in Harry's flat and the way he'd kissed me and murmured 'Diane'. Oddly enough – as I told Sven – now it all seemed rather remote and Harry a bit of an idiot. I mean imagine someone not knowing who they are kissing and I was such a fool to let him, knowing full well I didn't stand a chance.

I glanced at Sven sitting, jacketless and bare-footed on the floor, to see how he was taking these intimate revelations but he just listened impassively, now and then swigging from his glass of beer. His lack of response threw me a little but I rattled on – it was such a relief to talk to someone – about Giles finding my night things and the uproar that had followed with Giles chasing me to my room and Carla hysterically sending for her parents, ending with that extraordinary interview with Carla's mum.

When I'd finished he said. 'And that's it? That's why you ran away?'

I frowned. 'I didn't run away exactly.'

'Well you didn't give a week's notice either did you?'

'No but Mrs Markham accused me of deliberately stirring it.'

Sven fixed me with a candid blue gaze. 'Matty you did.'

Clenching my fist I thumped the arm of my chair. 'I was provoked!'

'Maybe,' he said quietly. 'But you didn't think of the consequences for Ned and Carla.'

I flopped back in the chair and closed my eyes. 'I know. You're right, I didn't.' And a couple of pricky tears wormed their way under my eyelids coming to rest on my cheeks. Poor Carla. Poor little Ned. What had I done to them? Mrs Markham was right. Sven was right. I'd put my foot in it again, only this time it wasn't glass or china I'd damaged, but the lives of people I'd grown to love, and one of them a small child.

'Oh dear,' I said and more tears sneaked out and I couldn't stop them so I just let them go. Then Sven took my hand and I slithered down into his arms and lay there bawling for the sins of a world in which I'd stupidly become entangled.

Eventually I stopped and Sven produced a box of tissues, so I blew my nose, wiped my eyes and took a gulp of his beer.

'If it's any consolation,' he said, 'the crunch would have come – sooner rather than later – without your help. Now they'll have to make up their minds what to do and that could be a good thing.'

I nodded miserably. 'I hope so. God I feel so guilty. If I'd known she was pregnant . . . '

'Giles is a bastard,' he said matter-of-factly.

'You can say that again.' I yawned. 'Do you know I've never stayed up all night before.'

He smiled and tucked a strand of wet hair behind my ear. 'Then I am initiating you into one of life's little pleasures. That's good.'

I giggled. 'That sounds a bit suggestive.'

'I know. I meant it to.'

Suddenly he was looking at me the way he had in June's flat, when I'd felt as though I'd been shot through with electricity and I realized it was happening again. I began to tingle all over and my breath got stuck somewhere in my chest. Sven just went on staring at me with this funny little smile, then leaning forward he took my face in his hands and kissed me lightly, but oh so lingeringly, on the lips. I just let it happen, but oh participate or anything, but when he stopped I felt amazing. Sort of shivery and hyped up.

'You are very, very sweet,' he said, 'but I am not going to make love to you tonight. You can have my bed and I'll take the chair.'

I nodded. 'Okay.' But neither of us moved: we just sat there holding hands and gazing into each other's eyes.

'I told you all about me when we met that afternoon in the park,' I whispered stroking the hairs on the back of his hand, 'but I know so little about you.'

He laid a gentle finger across my lips. 'You talk too much but you have a wonderful sexy mouth. It's driving me crazy.'

I grabbed his hand. 'That tickles, and don't change the subject.'

He gave a mock sigh and moved back a little. 'Well what do you want to know?'

'Everything. For example . . . ' I pointed at the cluttered desk. 'What's all that suff? Do you need it for your business?'

'No, I do that kind of business in the office.'

'Then what . . . ?'

'I am writing a book.'

'Wow! You must be very clever.'

He shook his head. 'No. I'm simply another sci-fi nut so I thought I'd have a go myself.'

'Little green men?'

'More sophisticated than that. I've even got a publisher interested.'

'Can I read it? I've never read a book by someone I know.'

He laughed. 'If it is taken I'll give you the first complimentary copy. It's nice of you to be interested. No one else is.'

'Not even June?' Well, her name had got to be mentioned sometime and it seemed the appropriate moment.

Sven shook his head. 'Specially not June. She has always hated my book.'

'Perhaps she's jealous and sees it as a kind of rival – something that takes you away from her.'

'You could be right.'

At the mention of June a constraint seemed to fall on us. There was so much I wanted to know yet was afraid to ask. I mean I'm not the sort who deliberately goes around looking for trouble and I'd burnt my fingers once already in the last thirty-six hours. Frankly I wasn't keen to repeat the experience but I couldn't help wondering what Sven had been doing in June's flat so late at night. I mean, were they lovers? Or not? June and I had never discussed their relationship in detail. We were not close enough. She was just that much older than me and, in spite of her disability, far more worldly. In fact I think she found me a bit of a simpleton although she was glad of my company when she felt lonely or just needed someone to gas to.

It was on the tip of my tongue to ask Sven outright but, when all was said and done, it was none of my business so I funked it.

Anyway, although he'd been given the opening, Sven wasn't volunteering any information and after a long silence he said, 'Where will you go tomorrow?'

'Home I suppose.'

'And then?'

I shrugged. 'I'll look around for another job.' I stared into the flames of the gas fire. 'Unless . . . '

'What?'

'Well, there is something but it might not work out . . . '

He didn't ask me what it was, he just nodded, as if I knew my own business best then he got up and began putting things into a travelling bag: shirts, pants, socks, the usual things.

'You going away?' I asked.

'Ya. Back to Stockholm. I have many meetings to attend.'

'For your paper-exporting company?'

'Right.' He opened a drawer and took out a crumpled bundle of clothes. 'I should have gone to the launderette. My mother won't be pleased.'

I gave a huge yawn. 'What's your mother like?'

He went on taking things out of the drawers and packing them into his bag. 'She's blonde and beautiful. Everyone thinks she is my sister.'

'Funny, that's the same with my mother.' I said sleepily. 'Perhaps they ought to meet.'

'Perhaps they will,' he said lightly. 'One day.'

Getting up I knocked off my shoes and stretched out on Sven's bed, hardly able to keep my eyes open any longer. 'Will you keep on this room when you leave?' I murmured. It suddenly seemed important.

He closed the bag and put it by the door. 'For a while but I'll be giving it up soon after I return.'

'Oh?' I wanted to ask why but my eyelids seemed incredibly heavy and anyway it was nice quietly watching him move around setting his things in order. Perhaps this was what marriage was like: just watching each other do ordinary things like washing and eating; going to bed and getting up. Good marriage that is, not one like the Robson's.

Sven came across and pulled a blanket over me, then he tucked it in at the foot of the bed and stood there looking down at me. His fair hair formed a sort of nimbus against the lamplight; his hands, resting on my feet, felt warm and strong.

'Sleep well Matty.'

'It's too late,' I murmured sadly.

'Of course it isn't. You've still got a couple of hours.'

'No I meant . . . ' But I couldn't remember what I meant except that it had something to do with Stockholm and Shropshire and the unbridgable distance between them.

Chapter 17

'So you've made a cock-up again,' Dad said by way of a friendly greeting at the station.

'P'raps you'd rather I got back on to the train?' I snapped. I mean he hadn't seen me for nearly four months!'

'Get in,' he growled, chucking my bags into the rear of the car.

We drove the rest of the way in silence; I was in no mood for playing the penitent little girl.

Parting from Sven had been bad.

'Don't get out at the wrong station,' he'd said through the open carriage window.

'I'm not that daft.'

'No? You could have fooled me.'

I grinned and hit him on the head with my magazine. 'Give my love to June. Say I'm sorry I didn't get down to see her in answer to her note.'

'What note?'

'The one she sent after that awful party. I wonder what she wanted.'

Sven peered down the platform. 'I've no idea.'

But he had. His nonchalant expression was a dead give-away. What's more, I sensed it had something to do with him, with them. Perhaps she wanted to tell me that he'd finally popped the question forced, no doubt, by her decision to go to the States. Come to think of it, that was obviously the reason he would soon be giving up his hotel room: he needed to buy his own place so that they could get married when she returned.

Sven gently tugged a lock of my hair. 'You've gone very quiet.'

I looked into his warm blue eyes – so different from Giles's glittering ice-cubes. 'I was just wondering if I'd ever see you again.'

'Of course you will,' he said. 'In fact I think I'll . . . '

'Excuse me!' A woman pushing an infant in a chair tried to shove past Sven to open the carriage door. Sven heaved the buggy into the train then he got in and put her bulging bags up on to the rack while she lifted the sleeping baby out of his chair and collapsed on to the seat.

'Thanks. I really thought we'd miss it. You wouldn't believe the traffic . . . ' Her round red face beamed with gratitude as she rattled on and on about nothing while Sven stood listening politely. I could have screamed with frustration.

Suddenly the train gave a jerk and Sven leapt off and slammed the door. As it slid out of the station he waved and shouted something I couldn't hear. I leaned out of the window and watched him getting smaller and smaller aware that I didn't know his address in Sweden or how long he would be away. Worse, I had no excuse at all for getting in touch with him.

I sat down and stared out of the window. I felt so confused by Sven's recent behaviour. What did he really feel about me? I tried to be realistic and convinced myself that he was simply a very kind friend; that he and June would soon be married and that he probably dismissed me from his thoughts before he'd even left the station.

'Don't look so sad,' the woman with the sleeping baby said. 'You'll see him again soon.'

I shook my head. 'I don't think so.'

'Tell you what . . . ' She pulled something out of the lapel of her jacket and handed it to me. 'I got this off one of those gypsies last year. White heather. It's supposed to bring you luck.' She kissed the top of her baby's head. 'It worked for me. You try it.'

'Thanks,' I said. 'I could do with a change of luck.'

I'd forgotten just how fantastic my home was until Dad drove down our lane, turned the corner and stopped the car facing the river. For a while we just sat looking, then Dad said, 'Better'n mucky old London eh?'

I nodded. On the opposite bank the trees, just turning from green to gold when I last saw them, now stretched their dark intricate bones up to a dull pewter sky. In front of us the wide, brownish river bubbled and swirled it's way through the dormant countryside. It was hard to imagine plunging into that hostile looking water in the heat of a summer's day. Even so it was the best thing I'd seen in months. Living in London had almost made me forget how the old place looked and felt. How beautiful, in fact, it was.

While Dad unloaded the car I went on a tour of the livestock. The cats, milling around the sheds waiting to be fed, immediately saw me as a potential provider and rubbed against my legs miaowing pitifully. I took it all with a pinch of salt. Cats are natural con-men. The bantams looked as entrancing as ever strutting around in their long feathered skirts. I gave them a friendly greeting but they ignored me. Barker and Corbett, Dad's golden Labs were more rewarding. They lumbered across the yard wagging and grinning like the amiable idiots they are, and made a great fuss of me.

Inside the house all was as quiet as only a pub can be out of hours. The kitchen was clean and tidy and the empty bar seemed to be resting before the busy evening. It smelled nice – a mixture of beer and tobacco and wood smoke.

I found Mum getting dressed for the evening session. She's a great actress and loves to look the part. In the mornings she likes to be the country woman, stomping around in wellies. At midday she can be found in the kitchen busy with the bread knife, sporting a whiter than white apron, and in the evenings she tends towards dramatic black and lots of make up. The local farmers love it. Mum knows the customers like a bit of glamour in the evening.

‘Hi pal,’ she said snaking into a slinky number with a plunging neckline.

‘Hi.’ I kissed her and plumped down on to the bed to watch her make up. Years of touring the clubs with her act made her an expert with make-up.

‘So what exactly happened?’ she asked eyeing me in the mirror. (Mum always gets straight to the point.)

I told her, leaving out the bit about Harry getting into bed with me, but keeping in the bit about Sven taking me back to his hotel. It’s odd the way you automatically censor things you tell people, so as not to make trouble for yourself.

‘Giles Robson sounds like a real four-letter guy,’ she said when I’d finished. ‘And Carla’s mother obviously isn’t capable of coping with the wicked world. She’d rather it didn’t exist in fact.’

‘Right.’

She outlined her lips with a pencil then grimaced at her reflection. ‘God I look a wreck! So much for the good life eh?’ She filled in the outline with a lip-brush. ‘Where do we go from here then? Any ideas?’

‘Yeah. I’ve thought about it a lot. I want to open a restaurant here, in the pub.’

Mum swung round on her stool. ‘You what?’

‘Something modest to begin with. Of course I’ll need to make a few changes. I can use the old dairy. It will take at least six tables and it’s right next to the kitchen. Naturally I can’t do it right away. I mean I’ll have to take a catering course first and I’ll need to raise a loan to buy the necessary equipment and make certain alterations to the kitchen. You can help me if you like.’

‘Oh can I?’ She sat there with her lip-brush in her hand staring at me as if I’d gone mad. ‘Are you serious?’

'You bet. Come on Mum, this place could be sensational if we offered really good food.'

'I don't know if your Dad wants it to be sensational.'

'You mean he's got no ambition?'

'No, I don't mean that!'

'What then?'

She swung back to the mirror and bared her teeth at herself. 'I don't know . . . It would be rather nice . . . Your grandmother always said you were a gifted cook but how am I going to persuade Dad that this isn't another of your little whims?'

'You're not,' I said getting off the bed. 'I am.'

As I left the room I caught a glimpse of her expression. It came as near to respect as I'd ever seen it.

Of course Dad wasn't easy to persuade. In fact we had quite a row. To start with he was dying to tell me off for quitting my job but finally agreed that with Giles and Carla's mother against me it would have been impossible to stay although, he said, I should have given in my notice properly. Then he pooh-poohed my idea about the restaurant saying he'd be stuck with it when I grew bored of the whole thing. On the other hand he admitted he'd been thinking about doing something about the pub's food but didn't know where to begin as it wasn't really Mum's scene.

I was as persuasive as I knew how to be: I'd given it so much thought; I intended to prepare myself properly, get professional advice, work my guts out, all I needed was the break etc.

'I don't know,' he said, gripping his pipe between his teeth. 'Two grown women using the same kitchen. It would be hell on earth.'

I laughed. 'You mean Mum and I would gang up on

you? Don't worry. I've thought of that too. We could convert the old stables into a bed-sit, kitchenette and shower-room and I could live there.'

He shook his head. 'I don't know. Folk would say I'd turned you out or something.'

'Oh Dad!' I moaned, exasperated. 'Take a chance for once. Do something a little daring and to hell with what folk say!'

He frowned, and for a moment I thought I'd gone too far but eventually he took out his pipe and knocked it on the stone hearth. 'All right. Let's give it a go.'

'Oh Dad!' I threw my arms around his neck. 'We'll bring 'em in from far and wide.'

He disentangled himself. 'You've got to start pulling your weight right now mind. No more messing. As from this moment the food is in your hands. Your mum can help if she wants but it's your responsibility. In the meantime you can apply for your catering course. I suppose it will be in London?'

'Dunno. I haven't had time to investigate. It's important to choose the right one.'

'God knows where the money's coming from. We'll have to talk to the bank about a loan.'

'They'll give you one won't they?'

'I don't know. We'll have to have the whole thing cut and dried. Figures, the lot.'

'Oh we will!' I could hardly believe my luck. Here were my parents actually listening to me and taking my advice. It made me feel amazingly grown up. It also made me nervous because although I'd said I'd thought a lot about this restaurant business, I hadn't. It had only been a vague idea before I left London but that conversation with Carla before my awful party must have gone home because when I finally talked to my mum it all just rolled out as if I'd planned it for weeks. Funny that.

'Have you ever been to Stockholm?' I asked Dad that night.

Unfortunately he hadn't.

The next morning Mum and I were just getting down to things in the kitchen when the phone rang. I picked it up.

'The Bluebell Inn.'

'Is that Matty?'

'Yeah, Carla, it's me.' I instantly felt apprehensive.

'Oh Matty I'm so glad. Are you all right?'

'Fine. Carla I'm sorry I ran off like that.'

'I don't blame you. God what a mess! I'm so sorry you got mixed up in it.'

'It was just what your mother said . . . '

'I know. She can't bear upheavals. I should never have sent for her. I panicked.'

'Well I shouldn't have said all that about Giles. It was awful of me.'

'Thank heavens you did. It explained everything. I thought I'd go mad not knowing what was wrong.'

'You're not angry with me?'

'Of course not. I only wish you were still here.'

I took a deep breath. This had to be said. 'I don't think I'll come back. You see I'm hoping to open a restaurant here, in the pub. I'm going to take a catering course first.'

'Matty that's terrific! We talked about it didn't we?'

I laughed. 'Yes. You inspired the idea. How's Ned?'

'Okay. He's gone down to the country with my parents. They get on like a house on fire.'

'But what about you and . . . the baby?'

'I'm all right. Don't worry, nothing's going to shift

this one. Giles and I are going to separate for a while. Who knows . . . ' she gave a grim little laugh. 'Perhaps absence will make the heart grow fonder. If not, well, I'll just have to cope. We won't be the only single-parent family in Chelsea.

'Carla I'm so sorry.'

'Well it's bad right now of course but it will get better. I think Giles will miss us more than he thought. Anyway I've got a good job and my mother will keep Ned until I can get someone to look after him and the baby. We'll have to move of course; this flat's far too big. By the way Harry wanted your address so I gave it to him. Is that okay?'

'Sure.'

'Let's keep in touch.'

'You bet.'

'I remember your beautiful pub so well. Do you do bed and breakfast?'

'No but if you'd like to come and stay . . . '

'Could we really? For a night or two, just Ned and I?'

'Great, we'd love it. Come soon after Christmas.'

'We will. Well . . . must go I suppose. Thanks for everything you did Matty.'

'Bye Carla. Take care.' She rang off and I sat there holding the receiver, all choked up and wanting to catch the next train to London.

After that I was pretty quiet, thinking of Carla and knowing the kind of life facing her if her marriage finally collapsed. Full time job, two tiny kids and no one to turn to when she was tired or miserable or ill. She'd need every ounce of courage she possessed.

'You all right love?' Mum asked once or twice, but I just nodded and went on making mayonnaise so she left me to brood alone.

The evening regulars were glad to see me.

'Well if it isn't the prodigal daughter!' Tom Knowles said plonking himself on his stool.

I bobbed a mock curtsey. 'Evening Mr Knowles. How's England doing then?'

He shook his head sadly. 'Terrible my dear. Terrible. Dunno what that fellow Botham thinks he's up to.'

'Never mind Tom,' Mum said setting up his special tankard. 'There's always another Test Match round the corner.'

He shook his head sadly. 'I dunno who'll want to play us after this.'

'Go on,' Mum laughed. 'Don't be so gloomy.'

'Matty,' Dad said, sticking his head around the corner of the bar. 'Someone wants to see you. I think it's that chap from London.'

Chapter 18

The glass I had been filling slipped from my hands, bounced off the counter and crashed to the floor. Immediately the bar fell silent and all eyes turned in my direction.

Mum laughed. 'Well London certainly hasn't changed Matty's luck, has it!'

I ignored her. 'Where is he?' I asked Dad.

'In the snug. Go on, don't keep the lad waiting.'

Half way down the brick passage I slipped into the ladies' loo to give myself a breather. In the mirror my eyes looked distinctly wary and my hair seemed to be standing away from my head like a cat's fur when it senses danger. Harry! Who would have thought he'd follow me here? When he'd discovered that I'd left London without saying goodbye he'd obviously been upset enough to ask Carla for my address. Perhaps he finally realized that it was me he really loved and not Diane. Perhaps he'd decided to ask me to . . . to . . . well, I don't know, but whatever it was, what on earth was I going to say?

– Sorry Harry but I don't feel the same about you now –

Hm. Difficult.

Outside the door of the snug I paused and took a deep breath then I pasted a whopping grin across my face and went in.

'Harry! How fantas . . . '

The person standing at the window with his back to me turned.

'Sven!'

'Ya. I'm sorry . . . '

'No, you don't understand. I am so glad you're here.'

'I wanted to tell you . . . but that woman on the train . . . '

'Yes I know. You were so polite. I was going mad.'

'I did not feel so polite.'

'Oh well, it wasn't her fault.'

'No but I wanted to say many things and when the train had gone I knew I couldn't return to Stockholm without seeing you again.'

I uttered a breathless little laugh. 'So . . . here you are.'

'Ya.'

We stared at each other. He looked so big in the tiny,

over-furnished room. A blond, bearded giant in a doll's house.

'Everything is as beautiful as you promised,' he said looking out of the window. 'London seems very far away.'

'Right. You'd never guess there were only five shopping days 'til Christmas.' I joined him and together we peered at the river swirling darkly under the flood-light Dad had fixed up on the bank.

'In Sweden we celebrate Christmas Eve in style,' he said. 'We have a party that goes on most of the night and we eat and drink to our heart's content. Everyone is happy. You will enjoy it.'

Was I hearing things? He must have meant 'would' not 'will'.

'It sounds amazing.'

'My family are expecting you.'

No, I thought, it's time to stop all this. How could his family be expecting me when they didn't even know of my existence? And what about June? I mean was this a private party or could anyone join in?

'Sven . . . '

'I know,' he interrupted. 'Before deciding anything we must talk so let's get comfortable.' Taking my hand he led me to the saggy two-seater in front of the glowing fire. He took up most of the room and I squashed in beside him.

'Now,' he said, 'Where shall be begin?'

I pleated a bit of my skirt. Now that we'd reached the critical point it was difficult. 'Well, I er . . . I mean what about starting with . . . '

'June?'

I nodded.

'Okay. Well June is planning to stay in the States

after her operation. Her father wants her to help manage one of his art gallerys in New York when she is fit. She's very thrilled. After all she has had plenty of experience.'

'Oh Sven!' I clutched the sleeve of his thick, Scandanavian sweater. 'You'll miss her. I'm so sorry.'

He looked surprised. 'Why? I am very glad for her. At last she will be doing something sensible. She has always been far too dependant on other people. Her father is giving her a chance to, literally, stand on her own feet.'

'But she'll never stick it out. She couldn't stay away from you that long. Don't you know she adores you? That's the whole trouble.'

'You are quite wrong. June doesn't adore me. Until now she has needed me – which is very different. She looked on me as a sort of a get-away car to marriage and freedom.' He gave a dry laugh. 'Mrs Belasco saw me that way too.'

'But you must have loved her to stick around when she was so moody and bad-tempered and everything.'

'Of course I did – once. But I'm fairly easy-going and I don't want a lot of hassle in my private life. It's bad enough in the office.'

'Then why didn't you break away?'

'How could I? The one time I tried she made herself ill and threatened to do terrible things.'

'What kind of thing?'

'You can imagine. Injure herself and so on. I didn't want any of that on my conscience. I admit it was not brave of me.'

'But that was blackmail.'

'No, it was a kind of game – rather a desperate one. She loved to put me to the test – to see just how far she could go before I got angry. I suppose the powerful feeling it gave her was a heady contrast to her real-life situation. Poor June. She is very insecure. She liked to quarrel in public but expected us to make passionate love when we were alone.'

I looked him dead in the eye. 'Is that what you'd been doing that night before you found me and took me back to your hotel?'

'No. We had spent the evening calmly discussing June's future. In the end we agreed it would be better if she left for the States free of all emotional ties. We even got a little drunk. To be honest I think we were both quite relieved it was over.'

'Oh well,' I said cheerfully, 'I don't really understand June. I can't play games with people. I either like them or I don't.'

'And you like Harry?' Sven said quietly. 'Even though he likes someone else?'

The knife between the ribs again. Why did I always leave myself open?

'I did,' I admitted slowly, 'but that's all changed now. I mean I still like him but I don't . . . well, you know, fancy him.' I didn't add that the reason was simple: I'd fallen out of love with one guy and in love with another. People have been doing it since the year dot.

He nodded gravely then he said, 'Christmas. You'll come won't you?'

'Why? I mean you've just ended a long-standing relationship; don't you want a break from girls?'

He laughed. 'That's the last thing I want! Anyway my real relationship with June ended months ago but it would have been wrong to break it off abruptly. I may be rotten but I'm not that rotten. I had to wait until she was ready.'

'Yes, I see that but . . . '

'My relationship with you began that day in the park. You were unlike any girl I'd met, either here or in Sweden – spontaneous, warm, natural and amazingly attractive.'

'Promise me something?'

'If I can.'

'When you get fed up with me you'll tell me instead of trying to be nice?'

'But you're different.'

He was busy tracing patterns on the palm of my hand and I shivered from head to toe.

'No I'm not,' I whispered. 'Sometimes I'm awful.'

He chuckled. 'You do seem to have a gift for upsetting things.'

'I know. Mum calls it Matty's luck.'

'I think we can change that,' he said, and drawing me close he looked deep into my eyes and I could feel myself trembling and longed to be kissed. At first he just feathered his lips teasingly across mine as if anticipating pleasures to come, and his beard felt soft and tickly at the same time; then he really kissed me, and I kissed him back, and I heard myself making funny little noises in my throat then, suddenly, he stopped kissing and held me close so that my head rested on his shoulder and his scratchy sweater was grazing my cheek.

'I love you Matty,' he said in my ear. 'Please come to Sweden.'

I sighed, happy yet troubled. 'I want to Sven, but I've made a bargain with Dad. We've agreed that if I work hard over the next few weeks he'll pay for my catering course and set up a small restaurant here in the pub. I can't go back on my word.'

'Just three days. It isn't a lifetime.'

'I dunno.' I sat up so that he could see I was serious. 'I've got to prove that I'm capable of following something through instead of copping out when it suits.'

He got up and began to wander round the little room examining everything from Mum's sheet-music lying on the piano to the family bible on the Welsh dresser.

I watched him, my heart in my mouth in case he failed to understand, but when he glanced round we smiled at each other as if sharing a tremendous secret and I knew it would be okay. Once I'd met Sven how could I have gone on wanting Harry? It was laughable.

In fact I must have laughed aloud because he came over and said. 'What's the joke?'

I shook my head. 'It's nothing. I'm happy that's all.'

'Would you be happier if we could spend Christmas together?'

'Of course but . . . '

'Wait. Do you think your father would like a pair of extra hands over Christmas, and if he got them would he let you off for three days over the New Year?'

'You mean you . . . ?' Jumping up I flung my arms around his neck. 'Oh Sven what a fantastic idea! Let's ask him.' I tried to pull him towards the door but he stayed his ground.

'Don't be in such a hurry. First we have something more important to do.'

'What? I mean what could possibly be more important than getting you and Dad together?'

But as his arms enveloped me and his lips touched mine I knew exactly what he meant.